ELLEN ELIZABETH HUNTER

MURDER ON THE
ICW

Magnolia Mysteries

www.magnoliamysteries.com

Published by:
Magnolia Mysteries

This is a work of fiction.

ISBN 0-9755404-4-0

Cover and book design by Tim Doby

Also by Ellen Elizabeth Hunter

Murder on the Candlelight Tour

Murder at the Azalea Festival

Murder on the Ghost Walk

Murder at Wrightsville Beach

Visit Ellen's website,
www.ellenhunter.com
Or contact her at:
ellenelizabethhunter@earthlink.net

Dedicated to the memory of
Finley Middleton
Beloved by family and friends

ACKNOWLEDGEMENTS

Dear Reader,

I am so enamored with Wilmington that I write about it as a real place, with the exception of a few fictional sites. The tiny peninsula I describe as being located on the Intracoastal Waterway north of Bradley Creek, home of Increase Boleyn's hunting lodge, is imagined. So too are Joey's Place, Ashley's home, Melanie's home, and Jon's home.

The restaurants I write about that make my mouth water are real. Try them. And no, I do not get paid for writing about them nor have I been provided one free meal. If only—

Officers Leon George, Samuel Lilly, and H.G. Gulley are historic figures, law enforcement officers who were assigned the thankless job of enforcing the Eighteenth Amendment and the Volstead Act. Lilly and George, and George's pet airedale Laddie, were ambushed and gunned down in an isolated area of Northwest Wilmington by the Stewarts, moonshiners who were later electrocuted for the murders. Gulley lived under a death threat that included his wife and children.

Thanks to some wonderful and talented friends, I am able to write and produce these books. There's Beverly Tetterton, Special Collections Librarian, North Carolina Room, New Hanover County Library who steers me in the right direction. Tim Doby designs the books and comes up with the right color combinations for the covers. He is a talented artist!

But it is you, my wonderful readers, who keep me going.

All the best,
Ellen

1

My sister Melanie is stalking a man.

The man is Joey Fielding, one-time television actor, now restauranteur.

Melanie is Wilmington's star realtor and the prettiest girl on the Carolina Coast. She is a former Miss North Carolina, representing our state in the Miss America pageant when she was twenty-one. So stalking a man is not something you'd expect her to do, not in your wildest dreams. Nor in my wildest dreams.

Melanie can have any man she wants. Since junior high, she has had her pick of the entire male population. As early as seventh grade, boys flocked to our front yard like starlings, dropping their bikes on the lawn like so much starling detritus before heading to the deep front porch where Melanie held court. Mama and Daddy were driven to distraction. The theatrics unfolded like the Twelve Oaks party scene from *Gone With the Wind* — Mama's favorite book — where Scarlett's suitors buzzed around her like bumble bees at a hollyhock bush in full, sweet bloom.

When Melanie's beaux grew into men, the pressure grew

— marriage proposals, expensive gifts, offers of exotic trips — nothing was too good for her, or too costly. With Melanie, men were usually willing to put their money where their hearts were.

Why then were we now stalking Joey Fielding? I say "we" because I had been recruited to accompany her on this recent descent into temporary insanity. I could not let her go alone; somebody had to save her from herself.

"I just want to see where he lives," she explained as she accelerated down South College Road on Wednesday afternoon. We were travelling in her recent purchase, a CLK 500 Cabriolet Mercedes convertible, identical to the car Joey Fielding drove. He has the best taste in cars, she had explained.

The convertible's top was down. The first week of November was unseasonably warm, as balmy as summer, temperatures climbing into the low nineties by midday, a not infrequent occurrence here on the Carolina Coast.

"But you already know the Monkey Junction apartment complex," I protested. "You know every piece of real estate in this town down to the precise square footage. So why do you need to see this complex?"

She turned to fix me with a frown. I couldn't see her eyes, hidden as they were behind a pair of oversized Holly Golightly sunglasses, but I knew they'd be narrowed, green irises flashing through long black lashes.

"Watch the road!" I screeched as we almost sideswiped a monster SUV. On my side too!

"I want to see which apartment he lives in, check things out," she argued with an atypical whine in her usually pleasant voice as she stomped on the brake for a red light at the intersection of Piner Road.

"And what if he's there? What if he sees you? We aren't exactly inconspicuous in this red car with your red hair." I glanced at her bright auburn hair. Mine is dark brown, not as showy.

"He's not there," Melanie replied with assurance. "He's at the restaurant."

"And you know this how?" I asked, exasperated. The entire subject of Melanie's obsession with Joey Fielding made me tired and cranky. I had love problems of my own.

I am Ashley Wilkes, historic preservationist. Together with my partner, architect Jon Campbell, I restore old houses in the Greater Wilmington area. And right now, we had a really big project underway that required all of my time and attention. Plus my own love life was in shambles with my marriage sailing down the tubes.

Yet here I was, racing toward Monkey Junction in a bright red, open convertible with my flamboyant red-headed sister who was as lovesick as a mare in season, preparing to scope out Joey Fielding's apartment. What idiocy! The outside of the apartment would look like any other, so what did Melanie hope to learn?

"I know he's at the restaurant because I checked the parking lot and his car is parked near the rear door," she replied to my question.

I had visions of my sister skulking around among the dumpsters in the parking lot behind Joey's Place.

"Besides," she continued, "I called the restaurant and asked to speak to him and when someone went to get him, I hung up. So I know he's there and he'll be there until after midnight. That's when the suppliers make their deliveries. I've seen the food trucks unload well after midnight. That man is so committed. He works as hard as I do and I admire that."

Now that was true. Melanie is thoroughly dedicated to her career.

"Melanie, are you telling me you spy on him in the middle of the night?" Oh, this was far worse than I had realized.

"Well," she said, going on the defensive, "I might have swung by there once of twice when I was out late."

Uh huh, I thought. Oh, Daddy, I wish you were here. I need you to help me handle her. But Mama and Daddy now reside in heaven, Daddy departing when I was a freshman at Parson's School of Design, then Mama following a mere three months ago. They were reunited there, I knew. They'd left us girls behind to fend for ourselves but it now seemed neither of us was capable of doing a good job of that.

"The last time I saw Joey Fielding was during last spring's Azalea Festival," I said. "You were showing him houses in the historic district. And Jon and I toured the Murchison House on Third Street when it was the Designer Showcase House with you two, remember? I thought Joey was going to buy an old house and hire me to restore it for him. That's what he said. But nothing came of that promise."

Melanie executed a sharp right into an apartment complex at Monkey Junction. "When Joey's TV show was cancelled," she explained, "he decided he wanted out of show biz altogether. And I can't say I blame him. It's a risky business for an actor. So he took his earnings and I found him the perfect piece of commercial property on Harbor Island near the Wrightsville Marina. He remodeled and I got him a great designer. The restaurant is fabulous. Celebrity-owned eateries are big drawing cards. Plus he had the good sense to pay top dollar for a fine chef so the cuisine is superb. The yachts pull in and tie up and they attract the tourist crowd. Now he's got a huge success on his hands. And I helped him accomplish that. But is he grateful? No!"

She whipped into a parking slot. "His building," she breathed, eyeing the towering three-story structure. With the motor idling, she put the car into park, then draped her arms over the steering wheel as she leaned forward. "Remember that song, 'On the Street Where You Live'? I know what that man was feeling, strolling back and forth in front of Eliza Doolittle's house. Why, I feel better just being here where Joey lives."

"Melanie, what is wrong with you!" I practically shouted. "I've never seen you act so pathetically. Aren't you embarrassed? What happened to your pride?"

"Oh, pride, schmide!" she declared hotly. Then she surprised me by wailing, "He's dropped me, Ashley. He won't even return my calls." She turned on me suddenly, yanking off her dark glasses. Tears swam in her green eyes, making them sparkle. "And I'm so crazy about him. Oh, he's nice enough when I'm in the restaurant, always comes over to my table and chats. He seems so happy to see me. But he never makes a move in my direction."

She balanced the glasses on her nose and peered at me over the tops. "We worked so well together, had so much fun, finding the right property, the right decorator. He flirted outrageously with me. And, well ... we got close. Now he treats me like I don't exist. Not even a dinner invitation. Every time I thought we were headed somewhere, he'd back off. Oh, it is all just so frustrating!"

She beat the steering wheel with her fists.

"I'm sorry," I said. I knew just how she felt. Hadn't I spent a year yearning for Nick until finally fate threw us together and we began the love affair that led to our marriage?

"What's wrong with us Wilkes girls?" I asked. "Have we got longing confused with loving?"

She gave me a level look. "Things aren't working out for you and Nick, are they, baby sister?"

"No. The atmosphere in my house is as chilly as a subzero refrigerator."

Movement caught our eyes and we looked up. Two girls came out of the second-floor apartment directly across the breezeway from Joey's apartment. Wiggling and giggling they descended the open staircase.

"Joey's neighbors," Melanie whispered. "And look at them, will you?"

The girls seemed young even to me and I'm only twenty-six. At the most they were nineteen, sun kissed and gorgeous. They had beach towels draped from their arms and beach bags slung over bare shoulders. They wore bikinis and high-heeled slides. Lip gloss and sun lotion. And nothing else. Long shiny sun-bleached hair bounced around their shoulders as they sashayed nubile bodies across the parking lot in our direction. They looked like freshmen from UNC-W.

They eyed the car, identical to Joey's which they surely would recognize, then they approached us. "Looking for someone, ma'am?" the blonder of the two asked Melanie.

"Is this Joey's car?" the other inquired.

"Uh, no," Melanie replied, pushing her dark glasses firmly onto the bridge of her nose with a perfectly manicured fingertip. "Just turning around." She tossed them a little wave, shifted into reverse, and backed out of the slot.

"Let's get out of here," she groaned as the girls clopped off toward a sparkling aqua pool.

The Mercedes sped out of the complex with a deep-throated purr and the squealing of tires. "'Ma'am!' The nerve of that skinny-assed hussy. She called me 'ma'am.' This is what I was afraid of. Joey's set himself up in an apartment with coeds for neighbors. Oh, now I'll never get him back. How can I compete with that? They're ... so young."

And to my surprise, she started to cry. Melanie never cries. Melanie is brave and strong, she is single-minded and focused. So who was this alien-being that had invaded my sister's body? Not my popular, exceedingly confident sister. Somehow Joey Fielding, who wasn't that exceptional in my opinion, had succeeded in doing what no man had ever been able to do: turn the unattainable Melanie Wilkes into a whiny, sniveling door-mat.

I wanted to grind him to pulp under my heel, crush him for the insect that he was.

"Pull over," I commanded. "You're in no shape to drive. I'm driving and I'm taking us for a drink."

"Now what did you mean when you said that you and Joey Fielding 'got close' this summer?" I asked over tall, icy Vodka tonics. "Melanie, you didn't have an affair with him, did you?"

She hesitated, then had the good grace to look guilty to be caught in an indiscretion. "He was too cute to resist." She smiled, remembering, then lifted her glass and took a long swallow.

The sun was setting and with it the temperature was dropping. I hate the way the sun goes down early in November, especially after we switch from Daylight Saving Time. I miss summer's long-shadowed long evenings. I'm a summertime girl. Born in the summer; love the summer.

We were sitting outdoors on the patio at Boca Bay on Eastwood Road, enjoying the last of the daylight. A small waterfall splashed pleasantly off to the side; colorful koi circling happily in a koi pond.

At first I'd wanted to take Melanie to the Bridge Tender Restaurant so we could have our cocktails out on the deck overlooking the Intracoastal Waterway. But the Bridge Tender is directly across the channel from Joey's Place, in clear but distant sight, and with her predilection for spying on him, I worried that Melanie might whip out a pair of binoculars from her purse and scan Harbor Island for glimpses of the object of her obsession.

"So you were sleeping with Joey at the same time you were sleeping with Mickey Ballantine," I accused. I always knew Melanie's "anything goes" philosophy where men were concerned was going to get her in a jam one day.

"Well, what do you care? You disliked Mickey with a passion. Remember?"

It was true. I did not like Mickey Ballantine. "Bad News Ballantine" was my name for him. And even though I owed him a debt of gratitude, that didn't cause me to suspend judgement and trust him. Mickey Ballantine, as I'd warned Melanie often enough, was bad news. And now it appeared Joey Fielding was bad news as well.

"I wasn't exactly sad to see him leave town, if that's what you mean," I replied.

Melanie got busy stirring her drink with a swizel stick. Her silence spoke volumes.

I pushed forward in my chair and glared at her. "No! Please do not tell me Mickey's still around."

Melanie glanced heavenward as if for help.

"But the police want him. Mel! There's a warrant out for his arrest. The police aren't stupid. They know he was running illegal gambling from his nightclub." I regarded her shrewdly. "So where's he hiding out? Do you know?"

"I might," she said slowly. "But don't misunderstand, Ashley. I am not seeing him. You were right about him all along. He is trouble."

"With a capital T," I said. Then a dreadful thought occurred to me. "Does he happen to know that you were having a thing with Joey Fielding at the same time you were seeing him? Because, Melanie, Mickey is not the kind of man to stand for that. He'd seek revenge. It would be a matter of honor with him."

No good will come of this, I told myself, and tried to quell the gut-wrenching premonition that trouble — real trouble — was homing in on us as stealthily and inexorably as a man-eating shark.

For a second Melanie looked alarmed. "No," she said thoughtfully, "I'm sure he doesn't know."

"All right," I said, "so why can't you let go of Joey? He's not that special. And he's a kid compared to you." Joey was nice enough looking, well-built, brown hair and brown eyes. A heart-stopping smile. Serious cheek bones. He had been part of an ensemble cast on the popular *Dolphin's Cove* series that had been produced and filmed right here in Wilmington by Cam Jordan, another of Melanie's besotted admirers.

Melanie got all huffy. She is eight years older than I, thirty-four to my twenty-six, but doesn't look a minute over thirty. And we don't look a bit alike. Melanie takes after Mama with her creamy complexion, green eyes, and auburn hair. I look just like Daddy with my serious, problem-solving expression, dark curly hair, gray eyes, heart-shaped face.

"Sorry," I said. "You know what I mean. He's not really man enough for you. You belong with someone like that adorable Cam Jordan. He operates on your level. And he's nutty for you."

"Cam is all right, I suppose. How can I explain it? Joey got to me in a way no man ever has. I don't know how. Or what happened exactly. Except that it tears me apart that we are not together. I can't believe he doesn't want me. I've never had a man not want me." She looked away from me, tears dancing in her eyes. She was really hurting.

The waiter approached. "Will you ladies be joining us for dinner?" he inquired politely.

"Yes," I said, looking up into his friendly, open face. He made eye contact and gave me a wide smile. Cute. A couple of years younger than me. But I was in too much pain over my failing marriage for even the lightest, most innocent flirtatious exchange.

"Want to share a sushi tray?" I asked Melanie.

When she nodded, I said to him, "That's what we'll

have." But I doubted I'd be able to eat much, just a few nibbles. I seemed to be existing on nibbles of food these days. The waiter moved to the next table, party of two couples, comfortable, in their sixties.

Melanie had seen the admiring way the waiter had looked at me and my lack of response. "Okay, so what's going on with you and Nick?" she asked.

I lifted my empty glass so that the waiter could see I wanted a refill. If I was going to discuss the subject of how bad things were at home, I needed fortification.

2

The collector from the Raleigh Bottle Club looked startlingly like Brad Pitt, short blonde hair, upturned nose, big blue eyes under sandy lashes and brows. I'm a girl, I can't help noticing these things.

Jon may not have noticed but if he had, it wouldn't matter to him. Jon is as straight as an arrow.

The bottle club member — his name was Derek Olsten — offered a dry handshake, firm but not gripping. I hate it when men crush the bones in my hand as if they are trying to impress me with their strength.

Right off, I sized him up as a man's man. He was dressed casually in a clean white tee shirt and faded denim bootcut jeans with scuffed brown boots.

"I brought an associate," he told us and motioned to his friend who was stepping down from the driver's side of a tan Durango. He nodded politely to Jon and me. He was about the same age and size as Derek — a bit chunkier — similarly dressed but not nearly as good looking. Both men wore gold wedding rings.

"Meet my cousin Clyde," Derek said.

Clyde shook hands formally, said how'd-ja-do politely. Clear blue eyes. Big smile. Country boys. The best.

"Where are the bottles?" Derek asked eagerly. "Sorry, don't mean to be rude but I can't wait to get a look at them."

Excitement was what I had heard in Derek's voice when I'd telephoned him early on Wednesday morning several hours before my adventure in covert operations with Melanie.

I had introduced myself and explained that my partner, architect Jon Campbell, and I were restoring a hunting lodge and that we'd found a treasure trove of antique bottles in an outbuilding we were preparing to demolish.

"We didn't feel we could simply cart them off to the landfill," I said, "and the owner is not interested. I knew they'd be important to someone, collectors like your club members."

"Yes ma'am, you were right to call us. And we appreciate it. Our club members organize digs in your area. Wilmington is a gold mine for antique bottles. Describe your find to me," he'd said over the phone, barely suppressing his excitement.

"The bottles are old, made of thick glass, not thin and clear like contemporary glass, but heavy glass, and somewhat opaque."

"Are there any colored bottles?" he'd asked.

"Oh my yes. Most of the larger bottles are dark green with blob tops. There's amber, cobalt, and amethyst. Some of them are round like canteens, others are flat flasks. And they are embossed," I added.

"Any guess how old they might be?" he asked with an intake of breath.

And because I know about such things as the ages of glass, I had replied, "I'd say about a hundred years old."

Derek had let out a long, low-pitched whistle and I'd jerked the phone away from my ear for an instant.

"There are quite a few mason jars mixed in with the bottles," I said, resuming our conversation, "but we can just trash those if you don't want them."

"Oh, we take mason jars too. If they're old."

"Ummm, Derek, Jon and I have discussed this and we don't want the bottles to be sold. We'd rather not have someone make a profit off this find since we are making a gift of them. I suspect they are collector's items and I'd like to see them in the hands of a reputable bottle club and displayed for educational purposes. That's why I called your club, it has a good reputation. Is that okay with you?"

"Yes, ma'am, I ain't got no problem with that. In fact, I'm with you all the way. That's what our club is all about, educating the public and such. But don't let's count our chickens before they're hatched. I better wait to see just what you have. How's ten in the morning? Good for you?"

"Perfect," I said. I gave him directions to the hunting lodge and told him I'd look forward to meeting him.

Derek and Clyde arrived at the lodge a few minutes after ten on Thursday morning. The sun was already heating up the coast, slanting across Wrightsville Beach from the east, highlighting the golden marshes and the ramshackle hunting lodge we were restoring for our client. The finger of land — a tiny peninsula — jutted out into the waterway. At the water's edge, a gaggle of geese clacked noisily in the rushes. The grass was high and dry and as we tramped through it to the shed, a cloud of yellow butterflies fluttered up and floated around us as weightless as feathers. An omen? I confess to being a tad superstitious.

We had discovered the bottles on Wednesday morning. The padlock on the shed door had been badly rusted but was still intact and I had wondered aloud to Jon why the vandals who had wrecked the hunting lodge had not trashed the shed as well. Jon had speculated that perhaps the lodge had provided a more tempting opportunity for trashing. Or perhaps the vandals had been interrupted and were forced to flee.

But as rusty as the shackle and loop had been, the lock was not so easily prized apart and Jon had had to retrieve a heavy-duty wire cutter from the stash of tools he hauls in the back of his Escalade. Once unfastened, the sagging double doors refused to budge. They had settled into the ground. We'd tugged and yanked, and finally a bottom edge splintered and gave, plowing a wedge in the dry and dusty earth as we'd dragged it toward us.

Inside we'd discovered the bottles. Hundreds of them, heaped up like a small mountain. Apparently just casually tossed in, one on top of the other, a mound so tall it reached my waist. Many were broken. Right inside the door a litter of glass shards had twinkled in the sunlight.

Now Derek helped Jon open the doors, grabbing the edge of one in a steely grip and yanking. Jon pulled on the other and together they spread the doors wide.

With the contents of the shed revealed, Derek stood silently gawking, lips parted, hands jammed in back pockets, feet spaced widely apart. "Jeez!" he exclaimed. Then, "Clyde, you gotta see this."

But Clyde had already moved up directly behind Derek's right shoulder, eyes widened, silent.

Derek leaned in and reverently lifted an amber bottle, held it up to the sky so that sunlight danced through it. "A strap-sided flask," he said. "Valuable." Then he lowered it to his upturned little nose and sniffed. "You can still smell it," he said as if he had been expecting nothing else. He passed the bottle back to Clyde who inhaled too and they exchanged nods of agreement.

Derek turned to Jon and me and grinned. "Moonshine.

Them's moonshine bottles. Corn liquor. Has a distinct smell. Originally they were legal distillery bottles or used for medicinals but during Prohibition they got recycled. Mostly, the moonshiners used mason jars, but they'd use any container they could get their hands on." He surveyed the estate, studying the several outbuildings, his roaming gaze halting at the derelict hunting lodge.

"Somebody made moonshine here once upon a time. And from the number of bottles in there, they made a lot. I'm assuming you've checked those other sheds."

"We have," Jon replied. "These are the only bottles."

Derek ducked his head. "Right. Just askin'. Okay, we'll back the truck around and start loading."

"Want me to give you a hand with the packing?" Jon offered.

"Thanks, but Clyde and me got it covered. Come prepared. Clyde, pull the SUV around, will you?"

Clyde left and headed back to where the two-ton Durango was parked, turned it around, then backed slowly over the long reedy grasses. A quail shot straight up out of the grass like a NASA rocket out of the Kennedy Space Center and took flight.

Distantly, the shrill warbling of a siren interrupted the peacefulness of the morning. "They're raising the drawbridge," I commented, referring to the drawbridge that connected the mainland to Harbor Island.

Greenville Sound was lovely in the fall; the blatant colors of summer had faded and mellowed into a gentle seascape. South of us, Bradley Creek flowed into Greenville Sound. With our semi-tropical climate, summer-like weather could prevail until Christmas, a boon for recreational sailors and yachting enthusiastics. Glistening white watercraft bobbed in the slips at the Bradley Creek Marina.

Money Island, an acre of high ground where according to

local legend Captain Kidd had buried two treasure chests, humped up out of the water a short distance from the shore. Beyond it and the marshes, Wrightsville Beach with its colorful beach cottages formed a barrier island between the mainland and the Atlantic.

"We got lots of practice at this," Derek said as he and Clyde unloaded wooden crates from the back of the Durango. "'Course never had such a promising haul as this one."

A huge plastic bag yielded excelsior. They began the work of crating the bottles, spreading a layer of excelsior in the bottom of a crate, carefully settling a row of bottles on top of the finely curled wood shavings, spreading the next layer, placing a second layer of bottles, and so on, until the crate was full. Then they hefted the crate into the back of the SUV and started a new one.

Derek lifted his clear blue eyes to my own. "My grandpa used to help his pa make moonshine when he was a kid and he told me how it's done. You wanna know how they did it?"

"Sure," Jon and I said together, nodding our heads. Not that making moonshine was something I'd ever wondered about.

"Well, it ain't as easy as you'd think," Derek said. "Lots of hard work, in fact."

Clyde continued packing, a man of few words. They'd probably been best friends since childhood and doubtless Derek had spoken for both of them even then.

Derek said, "The origin of the word 'moonshine' means something like 'work done by the light of the moon.' New Hanover County was big into moonshine back in the twenties. They liked to set up deep in the woods or the swamps, preferably near a creek because they needed a cool water supply for the mash and the worm."

"Worm?" I said.

Derek grinned. "Not that kind of worm. See, they'd build

a big stone fireplace. That would hold the still. The still is a copper jug, big some of them, could hold up to one hundred or two hundred gallons. Then there would be pipes connecting the still to barrels. The barrels held the corn mash. They'd mix corn meal with sugar and yeast and warm water. You can have malt whiskey or rye whiskey or corn whiskey, depending on what you add. If they added juniper juice they got gin.

"So the mixture in the barrels would have to be stirred while it fermented. A big operation would have six to eight people out there stirring — men, kids, women with babies on their hips. Moonshining was usually a family endeavor."

"I don't like the idea of little kids being involved in that," Jon said.

"That's the way it was back then. So anyway, they'd make the mash and let it steep for about eight days till it got thick and soupy. Oddly enough, the mixture was called 'beer.'"

"Beer?" I echoed.

He nodded and chuckled.

"Then the beer was boiled in the still. It's the vapor from the beer that becomes the whiskey. The vapor rises through the thumper keg and into the worm. The worm lies in cool water so that the vapor condenses and drips into a bucket. And those drippings are the whiskey."

"Does sound like a lot of work," I said, musing about how easy it was for me to walk into any restaurant or bar and order a drink. What those folks had to go through just for their six o'clock cocktails.

Derek bent to pick up the last of the bottles. "Well, that's all of them. Mind if I take a look around before we leave. Some of the stills might have been left behind, in one of those outbuildings, maybe."

"Sure. Help yourself," I said. "What does a still look like? We might stumble upon one and not even know."

"Basically, it's a copper pot. A pipe will be attached to it, and the worm. The copper would have tarnished after all this time so it'd be green and blackish. If you do come across one, you'll have to dismantle it. It's against the law to possess an operational still."

He dragged his boot back and forth through the broken glass as if a valuable bottle might be lurking there unseen. "Well, guess we're done here," he said, almost sadly.

The sun passed behind a cloud and for a moment the glittering, reflective quality of the glass vanished and I was looking at an ordinary blanket of broken glass. I blinked. Was that a face peering up at me through translucent shards?

Derek stroked the shards with his boot one last time.

"Stop!" I shouted and pointed. "Look! There's ... someone ... something ... down there."

Derek started, withdrew his foot and leaned in. Jon, so attuned to me, stared intently at the bottom of the shed. If I saw something, there was something there to be seen, would be his attitude. Clyde, who had been securing the top of the last crate, stopped what he was doing and moved up to join us.

I laughed nervously. "It's just that ... I thought ... oh, Lord. There's a face down there." I crouched down and squinted into the layer of broken glass. There *was* something. If only. If only I had my heavy gloves. And then I realized that I did. I pulled them from my back pocket, slipped my hands inside the leather, and began pawing through the glass — gingerly so as to avoid a sliver of glass piercing my finger painfully.

I had not been seeing things. What I thought I had seen was real. A bony face looked up at me.

The moan that escaped my throat sounded anguished to my ears. I stood up. "We have to get the authorities."

No one said a word but three men whipped out three cell phones faster than I could unclip mine from my waistband.

3

The first detective to arrive on the scene was Homicide Detective Diane Sherwood with a uniformed officer in tow. Diane used to partner with my husband Nick before he left Wilmington PD to take an assignment with Homeland Security, followed by, to my chagrin, a move to the CIA.

"You've done it again, Ashley," Diane said accusingly as she strode from the Wilmington PD cruiser. She was dressed in a loose fitting camel jacket, brown tailored slacks, a man-tailored shirt in brown and white stripes. The loose-fitting jacket concealed a bulky weapon.

I wasn't biting. While it is true that my restoration of old properties sometimes yielded macabre findings, that was certainly not my fault. "Anyone who opened that shed and removed those bottles would have discovered that corpse," I said in my defense. "Don't blame me."

She arched an eyebrow and gave me a smirk as if to say: But you have a history of doing this.

"How do you think it got there?" I asked.

Diane lifted her soft brown wavy hair off her neck, then let it fall gently back onto her collar. "I doubt that he crawled in there to die like an old sick cat," she said with sarcasm, and gave her hair a shake. "Someone put him there. So we're assuming homicide. Sure is hot out here in the sun. And to think in a few weeks it'll be Thanksgiving. Okay, so fill me in: what happened here? Who owns this place anyway?"

I gave her our client's name and cell phone number which she diligently copied into her note book. Then I explained the situation about the shed and the bottles, and introduced Derek and Clyde who were eager to get back on Interstate 40 to Raleigh. A corpse was more than they had bargained for. Me too.

A dark blue van that resembled a hearse drove up the lane and parked near the police car. We would soon run out of parking places if any other vehicles arrived. Diane introduced the woman who got out of the van/hearse as Dr. Jamie McAllister, a forensic anthropologist on the faculty at UNC-W whose specialty was Human Osteology — the study of human bones. I knew Dr. McAllister by reputation but had never met her.

She must have left her laboratory at UNC-W immediately upon receiving word that her expertise was needed at a gravesite of old bones. Several students from the university had come along to assist her. Dr. McAllister did not look much older than her students and seemed much too young to have Ph.D. after her name. She had dark red hair tied up in a pony tail, a petite figure, and freckled milky skin. She could pass for sixteen. Bet she got carded everywhere she went.

As she was introduced to us she gave Jon a lingering appraisal that was so obvious she could just as well have shouted: I am woman, you are man!

Well, Jon *is* special. He's a real hunk with golden blonde hair, a ruddy complexion from working out of doors, and laughing brown eyes that shine with sincerity and truthfulness. He is tall and trim. Plus he's got this great personality:

funny, a bit shy with women, a little naive. Every woman likes a man who makes her laugh and who isn't Mr. Smooth. Every woman that is except my sister Melanie who has a thing for the slick bad boys.

Dr. McAllister and her team went to work and I was drawn back into the world of the macabre. She and her students gingerly scooped broken glass onto a tarp they had spread out near the entrance to the shed. With great care they removed the earth, using hand trowels and brushes.

Standing, Dr. McAllister informed us that it appeared a complete skeleton had been buried in a very shallow grave. "The bones are just barely covered with dirt. Over the years the earth has settled. I'm going to need to examine those bottles. They'll provide valuable clues about the environment of this burial site. So I'm sorry," she said pointedly to Derek and Clyde, "but I'm going to have to ask you to take the bottles to my lab and leave them there for a few days."

With arms crossed over his chest, Derek had been shifting from one foot to the other, clearly irritated and obviously feeling he was being denied his treasure.

Diane exerted her authority. "One of her students can drive with you to the campus." As if to soften the force of her intent, she smiled at the bottle collectors. "They'll be returned to you when they are no longer needed."

Jamie McAllister was quick to reassure them as well. "I won't need the bottles for very long. A week. Perhaps only a few days. I promise that we'll take good care of them and repack them just as you did. I'll call you when you can pick them up."

She shook hands with both of them and gave them a big smile and the men seemed mollified. "Well, okay, sure, anything we can do to help," Derek the spokesperson said. He seemed charmed by the petite anthropologist.

Diane recorded Derek's and Clyde's names and addresses before they left with one of Dr. McAllister's students. As the Durango bumped down the rutted lane, Diane also recorded their license plate number.

From somewhere across the water, sirens screamed. Not the hooting of the siren when the drawbridge is being raised, but the wailing of emergency vehicles. A fire? I wondered. So many homes on Harbor Island were being renovated, and the danger of fire during renovation was always great.

Dr. McAllister and her students set about separating bones from glass and earth. It would take them the rest of the day, she told us, and well into tomorrow. Items that related to the corpse itself — clothing, fibers, artifacts — had to be carefully exhumed as well.

Diane's cell phone rang and after she listened intently, she hung up and declared, "Halloween was last week so what in the world is going on? Two homicides in one day! And this second corpse is fresh."

Addressing me, she continued, "I'm leaving Officer Bentley here to secure the site. Please don't go near that shed until you get the say so from me." And with that she turned on her heel and marched off officiously to her next dead body.

"Maybe they'll tear the shed down for us when they're through," I said to Jon as we trailed through tall grasses to the lodge and our vehicles.

As we walked, Jon speculated about the corpse. "If the bottles are a hundred years old and were used during Prohibition, how long do you think they were in that shed? Seventy years? Eighty years?"

"And as the corpse was under the bottles," I remarked, "surely it's been there for the same length of time. I wonder who he was. Or she? Maybe there will be a wallet or some form of ID."

"It's possible he — she — died of natural causes and for some reason no one wanted to report the death," Jon speculated.

"I've got copies of deeds and tax records back at my house. I'll go through them and see who was living here when."

"Well, our work's on hold until they're done here," Jon said, and we both hated the interruption. Our client, David Boleyn, was a demanding man, a person who was used to calling the shots and getting what he wanted when he wanted.

"So, want to get some lunch?" Jon invited.

"I'd better not," I said. "I need to go home. Things are ... Besides I'm not hungry."

I looked up into his warm, caring face. I saw the need there, the need for me. I didn't dare think about this new complication in my life.

"Tell me," he said and reached out to grip my upper arms, as if he alone could hold me up.

"Things are difficult. We are being very, very polite to each other. Tiptoeing around, avoiding talking about what really matters. We're not resolving anything. Nick feels badly that he let me down, and I feel badly that he let me down." I shook my head and my hair which is growing longer brushed my cheeks.

"It's just not working," I finally admitted, facing the truth, maybe for the first time.

Jon studied my face intently. "You know I can't be objective about this, Ashley. So I'm not going to give you advice. But I do want to remind you that Nick has been out of your life more than he's been in it, and that's no way to live. He's your husband, for God's sake. Doesn't he know how lucky that makes him?"

He was growing angry. And frustrated. "If I ... . Okay, I'm not saying another word. I've said them all before. You know how I feel. Call me later, will you? I'll be at home."

"I will. I promise." With head bent and shoulders slumped, I walked to my white van. Jon drove behind me out of the lane to Airlie Road. I turned left. He turned right toward the waterway. Jon lives on Wrightsville Beach in a salmon pink stucco house that backs up to the marshes.

I live downtown on Nun Street in Wilmington's historic district in a gray, white, and red 1860 Victorian house with a cupola and strong Italianate influences. I love my home. Jon had helped me to restore it two years ago when I'd bought it.

Originally, the house had been built for a Quaker minister and his family. I have a plaque from the Historic Wilmington Foundation that identifies it as the "Reverend Israel Barton" house. Reverend Barton lived there from 1860 until 1893 with his wife Hannah and their nine children. With three bedrooms upstairs and one bathroom, it must have been a tight squeeze. Reverend Barton had been a staunch abolitionist and during his time my home had been a stop on the Underground Railroad.

As I passed the lacy wrought iron gates to Airlie Gardens, I couldn't help notice that the afternoon was breathtakingly beautiful, yet my dark mood would not permit me to take pleasure in the beauty around me. I was in a deep slump. As I turned onto Oleander, the tears started. "Our marriage is over," I whispered to myself, "and I don't know what to do to save it. Nick is lost to me."

I hoped that Nick would be at home when I got there; he had been away often recently. Sometimes for days at a time. And he never said where he was going or warned me when he would return. But I was determined to talk things out with him. It had to be done. I had to make one last effort, one last appeal to save my marriage. As I approached downtown and Nun Street, I promised myself I would maintain a light tone, I would not accuse, I would be reasonable.

Nick's SUV was parked on the street in the shade of a towering live oak. I parked my van directly behind his. As I climbed the porch steps, I stilled the rush of panic that threatened to consume me by concentrating on the ferns that flourished on my porch. I reminded myself to keep an eye on them and the weather. A sudden and surprise hard frost would mean the end of them if I did not take them inside. The unheated porch off the kitchen would make an ideal winter retreat for my frilly friends.

I opened the front door, about to call Nick's name to let him know I was home, but my voice died quickly in my throat. I wasn't prepared for what I saw inside the reception hall. Stacked neatly at the bottom of the stairs was Nick's luggage. My heart sank and one hand clutched my middle while the other reached for the newel post. It seemed like I was always saying goodbye to him.

I stood still for a moment, getting a grip on my emotions. I listened and heard his voice drifting down from the guest room where he'd been camping for the past month.

So he was leaving again. How could we ever resolve the problems in our marriage when he never stayed around long enough for us to work things out? I asked myself. But I already knew the answer. We couldn't. The man was a wanderer, a born adventurer. This was hopeless.

I didn't want a scene. I didn't want to become a nagging wife. I refused to plead with him to stay with me. It was clear he was leaving again and he hadn't even discussed it with me. Was he waiting for me to come home to tell me? Or did he plan to leave me a note? A note that would say something like, *Sorry, Ashley, I'm off again on another mission to make the world safe for democracy.*

I called his name softly and headed up the stairs. I stopped abruptly outside the open door to the guest room. I hadn't intended to eavesdrop but something about the quality of his voice arrested me. He spoke softly and lovingly, a tone I had not heard in a long time.

"I'll leave as soon as Ashley gets home. I have to tell her. But I'll drive like the wind to reach you before dark. We'll get some supper."

He chuckled softly. "Staying in sounds better to me too."

I stepped into the doorway just as he was saying goodbye. "I miss you, Carol."

Nick closed the phone with a snap, looked up, saw me, and our eyes met across the room. "Ashley," he stammered, clearly embarrassed. "How long have you been standing there?"

"Long enough to know you're leaving me for someone named Carol," I retorted angrily.

"I'm sorry you heard that. I wanted to tell you ... "He didn't finish but the expression that crossed his face could only be described as relief.

I held my breath. If I didn't breath, maybe I wouldn't feel. Feel the pain that I knew was about to punch the air out of my lungs. But it came anyway.

I let out my breath with a long, ragged sigh. There was something so final about the sound. Final and accepting.

"Tell me what?" I asked coldly.

"Ashley. I didn't mean for you to find out this way. I planned to tell you. This isn't working for me. You either, if you will be truthful. You aren't any happier than I am. I need . . ."

"Carol?" I asked in a whisper.

"Yes," he said softly, and lowered his head as if defeated. Then he lifted his eyes to mine. "But more than Carol. I'm not the kind of husband you want . . . need. I'm not a guy who can hang around the house, plant a garden, do domestic stuff like that. You knew that about me, Ashley. Don't look surprised."

"I'm not surprised," I said. "You're an adventurer. And what adventure are you chasing after now, Nick?"

"I'm joining Blackwater Security," he replied.

"And Carol? Is she a part of Blackwater?" I had crossed my arms around my middle, trying to hold myself together. Physically. Mentally. I wanted to scream. To launch myself at him and beat him with my fists.

The look he got on his face was dreamy as he spoke her name. "Carol is a K9 trainer there."

Oh, dear Lord, this was worse than I thought. He was in love with her.

"It's a fabulous place, Ashley. They've got six thousand acres in Moyok, North Carolina, and they're dedicated to supplying the best security forces the world has ever known."

"Supply to whom?" I asked.

"State and federal government. The DOD. Homeland Security. Friendly nations." He stretched out his arms. "Ashley, this is something I have to do. Forgive me."

And he strode out of the room without a backward glance. He did not kiss me goodbye, or hug me, or promise that we could be friends. Nothing. Goodbye. I'm gone.

I turn and fled, brushing past him in the upstairs hall. I heard sobs as if they came from another person. Back down the stairs, past his waiting suitcases. Let him leave! Let him drive like the wind to reach Carol and his new life. I wasn't staying to witness his abandoning me.

"Ashley! Ashley, wait!" he called after me, bounding close behind me down the stairs, out onto the porch.

But I was faster, driven by a hurt too large to face. Besides, he didn't really want to catch me. He wanted to be on his way.

He stopped at the top of the porch steps as I opened the door to the van. "I'm sorry," he called feebly after me.

I'll bet you are! I wanted to shout at him but didn't.

Somehow through my tears I managed to fit the key into the ignition, turn it, put the van into reverse, back up, then pull out into Nun Street.

I knew exactly where I was going. I was running to a safe place, a place I should have run to long ago. I grabbed some tissues and dabbed my eyes.

Then I drove back out Oleander toward the waterway and to Jon, my safe harbor. I think at that point I realized that my need for him was as great as his was for me.

4

I wiped away my tears and drove out of the historic district, got back on Oleander and headed for the beach. I had to think, to get a grip on my emotions. Face facts. My husband was leaving me.

Husband? Had Nick ever really been a husband to me? He used our home like a hotel, came and went like he was a hotel guest. He'd never treated our home as if it was the center of our life together, but a base from which he could make frequent trips. Work always came first. Even before we were married, while we were dating and falling in love, he had accepted a position heading up Atlanta PD's cold case task force, effectively ending our relationship until he'd been offered a better position as Homeland Security liaison officer back here in Wilmington.

Work. It was always work. Work had brought him back to Wilmington, not me. But he loved me, I had been sure of that. We married. He traveled and I remained at home, waiting for his return, working with Jon on old house restorations.

During the summer Nick had been on assignment with the CIA. I had not been able to reach him to tell him that I was expecting our first child, or that my mother had died. He'd been out of the country, on assignment in Baghdad — something I'd known nothing about — he had told me belatedly. That was what he'd admitted to me in my hospital room the day after I'd lost our baby.

Now, I thought, tears blurring my vision again, I didn't have our baby to love, and I'd lost Nick too.

I took a deep breath. I had expected more from him. Honor, for one thing. Fidelity, for another.

My temper flared, a hot flame that burned bright and made my chest hurt. I had to get a grip on myself. Okay, I told myself, so he doesn't want me. Am I the kind of woman who wants a man who does not want her? No way. I'm better than that. I deserve better treatment than that, much better! I want a man who considers himself lucky to have me in his life. And was that man Jon?

I turned onto Eastwood Road, and drove past Lumina Station, its architectural style a replica of the original Lumina Pavilion. There were shady trees, fountains, and white rockers. The familiar landmark helped to ground me. I knew every shop and restaurant in that shopping center.

Am I going to start acting like Melanie, I asked myself, heartsick over Joey Fielding who won't give her the time of day?

No, I had a life, doggone it! And a man, a real man, a good man, in love with me. Now I was running to him.

"I'm driving to Jon, Nick," I said out loud. "I've got the wind at my back and I'm speeding to him. Ha! I'll show you!"

Instantly, I felt guilty. Jon didn't deserve to be treated like a runner-up in a beauty pageant. He deserved a woman who put him first.

I'd been sailing along when all of a sudden I hit a wall of traffic and stopped just in time to avoid rear-ending the car in front of me. The drawbridge over the waterway must be up, I thought. But craning my neck, I could not see the raised ramp nor the masts of tall ships passing through. So the bridge was not up.

And traffic was moving, but only by inches. Perhaps an accident? Something had brought traffic to a snail's pace.

I'd been thinking about sparing Jon but had to acknowledge that nothing would make Jon happier than to have me fly to his arms. And how did I feel about him? Honestly. Being married, I'd never let myself think about having feelings for him that were greater than friendship.

He was my best friend. I'd always heard that those kind of relationships made the best marriages. To marry your best friend, how comfortable that must feel.

On one level I did love Jon. But we had never had the boy/girl thing between us. What would that be like? I asked myself.

I visualized Jon's handsome face, his golden blonde hair. In my mind's eye he was walking toward me and I admired his broad shoulders and trim waistline, his long legs. A sexy man. I recalled how his face lit up when he saw me. Then felt a rush of excitement at the prospect of responding to that joy.

So, there *was* chemistry between us. And I'd been suppressing it out of loyalty to Nick and faithfulness to my wedding vows.

I realized something else too. Every time Jon met a girl he liked and started dating, my initial reaction had been jealousy, which I had always quickly talked myself out of.

I inched the van forward but the line of traffic was making little progress. Glancing in my rearview mirror, I saw cars backed up to Lumina Station.

I acknowledged to myself that I had changed in the two years since I'd first met Jon, about the same time I had fallen in love with Nick. A girl changes a lot between the ages of twenty-four and twenty-six.

I knew that from personal experience. I was more comfortable in my own skin these days. Melanie, who had always seemed so out of reach when I was growing up, I now met on equal terms. I had matured since my graduate school days. I owned a successful business, and my mirror told me that I was better looking, the angularity of youth having been softened by womanliness.

Perhaps that meant I was now ready for a mature kind of love. The kind of love Jon could offer me that Nick could not.

Maybe it was time for Nick and me to move away from each other and move on to other partners. Surely, he had needs that were not being fulfilled by me, otherwise he would not have gotten involved with this "Carol" person. At the thought of Nick being with another woman, anger raged inside me like an out of control fire. The cheating made me mad! Especially since I had denied Jon and myself the closeness we both craved.

Well, all that was about to be rectified, I told myself with determination. I reached for the cell phone on the passenger seat to call Jon but it chirped just as soon as I touched it, as if my touch had set it off.

"Jon! Hi!" I said. "I was just thinking about you."

I felt my face flush. If only he knew how I'd been thinking of him.

"Ashley, where are you?"

Jon sounded frantic.

"Why, what's wrong?"

"I've been calling your cell but you must have been in one of those dead zones. Where are you?"

"I'm stuck in traffic on the bridge. I was just driving to your house, but now I'm stuck on the bridge and it's going to be a while before we get across."

"That's what I'm calling you about. There's been . . ." Static and lost words. ". . . so Melanie . . ."

"What? Jon I'm losing you! What about Melanie?"

I held the phone out and shook it. As if that would help.

"Jon! Jon!"

Gone. Dead phone. Melanie what? I wondered. What did Melanie have to do with this traffic snarl? Good Lord, no! Not an accident. I always knew her speeding would cause an accident.

I dialed her cell phone and got a busy signal.

I had made it to the center of the bridge. The Intracoastal Waterway stretched to the north and the south as far as they eye could see. Sunshine sparkled on the ripples. The sky was cloudless, and white sails billowed on blue water.

Mother Nature mocked me with her beauty.

I pushed the send button and tried Melanie again. The traffic ahead surged forward. I was glad to be in the right lane so I could exit the Causeway when I reached land.

"Ashley!" Melanie screamed, identifying me by my number. "I've been calling you and calling you."

So that's why her line had been busy.

"Where are you?" she shouted. In the background I could hear loud voices, a lot of people. A restaurant? She had not been in an accident after all?

"Melanie? Are you all right?" I asked.

"Oh, Ashley, you don't know what's happened. Where are you? You've got to get here."

I told her I was driving off the bridge onto Harbor Island.

"Thank God!" she exclaimed. "I'm here. At the Bitterman house. Come straight . . . "

I lost her.

The Bitterman house? On Harbor Island? "Where?" I asked. I was yelling, which we tend to do when we cannot hear.

Static buzzed in my ear.

"Oh for God's sake!" she cried. "The Bitterman house.

My listing on Point Place. You're almost . . ." Her voice faded in and out.

" . . . listened to me you'd know."

With Melanie, everything was always my fault.

"Okay, I know the house you mean," I said. "I'm almost there."

"Well, hurry! You can't imagine what these idiots . . ."

Again I lost her.

"Melanie, you're breaking up."

"Hurry, Ashley, . . . make the police let you . . ."

Then she was gone.

Police? What was going on?

Right before the bridge over Banks Channel, I cut a sharp right onto Channel Drive and immediately hit a police barricade. A uniformed officer motioned for me to turn around but instead I pulled over, got out of my car and approached him.

"Officer, I'm Ashley Wilkes. I just got a call from my sister, Melanie Wilkes, who is somehow involved in this . . . whatever is going on — what *is* going on? I've got to get through."

"No one's allowed in here, Miss. You have to leave. This is police business," the officer told me curtly.

"Oh, wait, there's Officer Meriweather," I cried. "Officer Meriweather!" I called to a second man wearing the Wrightsville PD uniform.

Meriweather turned and walked toward us.

Officer Hank Meriweather was someone who knew my family well. He had issued speeding citations to Melanie on many occasions, but mostly he'd lectured her about the risks of driving too fast for conditions. He was a good police officer, concerned with the well being of the citizens within his jurisdiction. He had been a friend of our father, the late Judge Peter Wilkes.

"Miss Wilkes," he greeted me soberly. "It's okay, you can let her through," he told his colleague.

"What's going on?" I asked Meriweather. "How is Melanie involved? Is she all right?"

"We've got a serious problem here, Miss Wilkes. Get in my car and I'll take you to her."

I removed the keys from the ignition, picked up my purse and cell phone, and got into the PD cruiser with Hank Meriweather. We drove onto Point Place where beautiful three-story cottages faced the water. Melanie had a listing here, the Bitterman place, as she had reminded me, with its own boat dock and worth several million dollars.

Skillfully, Meriweather maneuvered the cruiser between what seemed like every cop car in the Wrightsville PD's fleet, passed a fire truck and pulled up behind an ambulance. Melanie's red Mercedes was parked in the driveway. I was almost too scared to speak.

"What happened here?" I gasped.

The doors to the house were standing open; police officers searched the grounds and crime scene techs rushed in and out of the house.

Just then the paramedics came out, wheeling a gurney between them. On the gurney lay a fully zipped body bag. I stumbled out of the car.

"Melanie! Melanie!" I cried and ran toward the gurney.

Meriweather caught my arm. "Miss Wilkes, take it easy. That's not her. Your sister is not the victim."

I watched as the gurney was wheeled to the ambulance. The construction team from the house next door that was under renovation crowded in the street, watching too. A news van was parked there, a cameraman moving in for the kill, live cam balanced on his shoulder.

I turned back to the house and shock made my heart stop beating. Two uniformed officers were leading Melanie from the house. Her hands were cuffed behind her back.

The news camera captured her perp walk to the police car. I thought she would be embarrassed and mortified, instead she lifted her chin and glared defiantly into the camera.

"There's been a terrible miscarriage of justice committed here today," she declared hotly. "And I'm going to sue everybody involved."

Meriweather's gripe on my arm tightened, preventing me from going to her.

"Who is the victim?" I asked him.

"Joey Fielding. Shot in the head. Fatally. She's really done it this time, Miss Wilkes," he told me sorrowfully. "This is no traffic ticket I can fix for her."

5

What did the police know? Why did they think Melanie had shot Joey Fielding? These were the questions I asked myself as I followed the Wrightsville PD cruiser to the sheriff's detective division.

At the first stop light I picked up my cell phone and called Walter Brice, an outstanding defense attorney, and a friend of our late father. I was put through immediately and felt lucky that Walt was not in court. I explained the situation to him and he assured me he would meet Melanie at the Detective Division downtown and be present during her interrogation.

"She knows better than to say anything without me there," he reassured me. "Melanie is smart. And tough. So don't worry, Ashley, I'll take care of everything and if they arraign her I'll have her out on bail. I promise you. But it might not happen until tomorrow morning, so prepare yourself."

Melanie was no flight risk, that was a certainty. She had strong ties to the community. She was a billion dollar real estate producer, for pity sakes. If the D.A. was ever dumb enough to take this case to trial, he'd be hard pressed to find twelve jurors Melanie had not sold houses to or for. She was that well-known and that popular.

How could they think Melanie was capable of killing anyone? Oh, she was temperamental and headstrong. She had her own way of doing things — she was certainly not conventional — but that did not make her a killer. No way.

My next call was to Cam Jordan. Again I was put through right away. Cameron Jordan was the president of Gem Star Pictures which he had founded. I liked Cam. He was good for Melanie and I could never understand why she had dropped him. He'd moved to Wilmington from Los Angeles where he'd been the executive vice president of programming at HBO. He'd wanted out, he told us, wanted his own production company, and he built one too, and successfully, starting with the overnight sensation, *Dolphin's Cove*, getting it into production when no one else believed a series about a group of high school seniors could succeed. The others were wrong. The series had run for three years, actually rather remarkable for the fickle television industry. After L.A. and New York, Wilmington ranks third in the nation for the production of movies — and television shows, like the long running *Matlock* series that had been produced and filmed here as well.

"Ashley, hi! Long time and all that. I take it there is a purpose for this call," Cam said pleasantly.

Cam and I always had seen eye to eye, we'd shared an unspoken vow to look after Melanie.

"I assume you do not have the television news on," I said.

His voice grew alert and tense. "No. What's happened?"

I told him the bad news.

"Where are they taking her?"

I told him the Detective Division at Fourth and Princess.

"Okay, I'll meet you at there. I'm on my way, Ashley."

He was gone.

Jon called then. "I saw the whole thing on TV. Where are you, Ashley? Are you okay?"

"I'm almost downtown." I gave him directions. "I'm meeting Walt Brice there. And Cam Jordan."

"And me," he said. "I'm not far behind you. Wait for me there. Melanie will have Walt and Cam. But you, you'll need me. I'll be right there. Don't leave until I arrive. I'm taking care of you."

Dear, sweet Jon. What would I ever do without him? Then I realized that I didn't have to ever be without him. Nick, for all the pain he was causing me, was setting me free. Free to find the love I needed.

Hurry, Jon, I whispered to myself after we ended our call.

6

"I want to know exactly what happened," I told Melanie. "Tell me everything and no embellishments, please."

It was late Friday afternoon and we were in the master bedroom of Melanie's comfortable ranch house on Sandpiper Cove. She was in bed, resting from her ordeal.

And fuming. "When I get through with the judicial system in this town, they will be sorry they ever heard the name Melanie Wilkes," she declared. "Can you imagine? Holding me in lock-up over night! If Daddy were alive, they'd never treat me this way. He'd have their heads. I am boiling over with rage at this miscarriage of justice! While they are fixated on me, the real killer is out there, walking around, getting away with murder!"

Melanie's arrest on Thursday and her arraignment early Friday morning had the TV journalists quivering with excitement. The *Star-News* had devoted a double spread to the murder of Joey Fielding and Melanie's subsequent arrest for that murder while news of the skeleton we'd unearthed at the hunting lodge was buried on a back page. On TV the talking heads were going on and on about Joey Fielding's star status when he'd acted on the popular, long-running *Dolphin's Cove* hit television series.

"And let's not forget I've lost Joey," Melanie wailed. "That gorgeous, sexy hunk of a man is dead! What a waste."

"But why do the police think you killed him, is what I want to know," I said.

Melanie let out a groan and plopped back on the pillows. The ice pack she'd been holding to her forehead slipped down onto the satin coverlet.

"Because they're all idiots!" she exclaimed. "That's why."

"Okay, start at the beginning and tell me what happened."

But Melanie was not through venting. "You can't imagine how disgusting that jail cell was. Talk about dirty. And no privacy. Oh, someone is going to pay for doing this to me."

"Why don't I get you a glass of wine," I suggested. "Maybe that will help you to relax."

"There's a nice bottle of Pinot Grigio in the wine cooler," she replied, accepting my suggestion.

I left her adjusting the straps on her silk nightgown. "Ashley," she called after me, "bring the whole bottle. It's going to be one of those nights."

Crossing Melanie's serene living room-dining room, done in pale taupes and ivories with soft touches of peach and aqua, I recalled happier days. How we'd decorated these rooms together right after Melanie purchased the house the first summer I was home from New York and Parsons School of Design. We'd had so much fun shopping for the wonderful art deco pieces that blended marvelously with the fat Thirties-style Tuxedo sofas and club chairs. And we'd hung the filmy linen panels that fell in deep folds across the sliding glass doors that led to the terrace.

Over the fireplace an oil painting of a sunset at Wrightsville Beach was prominently displayed, a gift from

Cameron Jordan when he and Melanie had been dating. The painting was executed in brilliant colors. In it, the sky was layered in bold reds and pinks. The sun was setting in the west just outside the frame, shooting rods of flame across the sand dunes. Surprisingly the striking hot colors of the painting complimented the austere coolness of the room.

Melanie was meticulous about her surroundings, so particular that her environment be beautiful and arranged just so. How dreadful it must have been for her to be held in a jail cell over night. But Melanie, for all her prissiness, is incredibly strong. She had made it through the ordeal with her confidence intact, in fact she was feistier than ever, determined to make somebody pay for accusing her unjustly.

I was just glad Daddy was not alive to see his daughter arrested like a common criminal.

I collected the perfectly chilled bottle, two wine goblets, and the cork screw, and headed back to the master suite. Melanie was on her cell.

"Oh, darling, Cam, I can't thank you enough for coming to my rescue. I knew you wouldn't let me down. There are people in this town — jealous, small-minded people — who are happy to think the worst of me, but you'd never take that attitude."

She listened as he spoke.

I'd gone to the courthouse that morning to make arrangements to pay Melanie's bail money, but Cameron Jordan had beat me to the punch. Melanie was perfectly capable of paying her own bail, she had more money than I, but she'd let Cam pay her bail anyway. It was the principal of the act, his solid declaration that he believed in her.

And still loved her, I was sure.

Melanie had Cam wrapped around her little finger and it sounded like she was now rewarding him for his devotion. But I was glad he was back in the picture. Maybe some good would come out of this tragedy after all.

She clicked off the phone, smiling.

"That darling man. He is so good to me. He offered to take me to New York for a few days of fun, theatre and shopping." She frowned. "But because of those idiot police I can't leave town. So we're going out on his yacht for the weekend. Walt got the judge's okay. We can't go far — just cruise around the waterway — but it'll be fun. He is the sweetest thing." She smiled to herself and twirled a curl around a finger.

Was her obsession with Joey Fielding finally a thing of the past? I sincerely hoped so. Because with him dead, Melanie could really be stuck, frozen in time over a love that could never be. And Joey would assume larger than life appeal and she'd never get over him.

Then her expression grew steely. "But when I get back on Monday, watch out! Fur is going to fly, and it won't be mine."

I was pleased by these latest developments. "Cam Jordan was always gaga over you, Mel," I said.

"Yes, he was," she agreed, smiling slyly. What was she up to?

"Okay, little sis, so here's what happened on Friday. You know I have the Bitterman listing. And the Bittermans are at their new condo in Palm Beach. Bunny Bitterman asked me to personally keep an eye on the house for them and you know how I baby my clients. They've got valuable antiques and paintings in that house."

"Yes, I've been inside. I remember now. I attended a political party there when John Edwards was running for vice president," I said. "And everyone knows who Brie is."

"Anyway, I've been making a point of stopping by every afternoon to check on things and water the plants. Well, when I got to the house yesterday afternoon, the door was unlocked. I inserted my key to unlock it and discovered it was already unlocked. And I'm sure I locked up the previous day.

"I went inside the foyer, calling for Bunny and Clay, but felt sure they were still at Palm Beach. I thought Brie might have been there. I'd heard that she was back in Wilmington between tours."

Brie Bitterman was a teenage diva, only seventeen but wildly popular with the tweens and teens and at the top of the charts. A Grammy award winner. She had a manager who traveled with her on world tours.

"But going into the house alone wasn't smart, Mel. You should have phoned the police. There could have been a robbery in progress and you could have been hurt."

But Melanie has always been a risk taker.

She waved a hand in the air dismissively. She was just too headstrong for her own good. Then continuing her story, she said, "Lying right there on the tile floor just inside the door was a gun!"

"Oh, no!" Then I realized what was coming next. "And you picked it up!" I guessed.

"I did. I couldn't imagine who had left it there. Again I thought of Brie. Maybe her manager carried a gun and had somehow dropped it. I know that doesn't make sense but I just wasn't thinking clearly.

"So I picked it up and set it carefully on the hall table, then went in search of whoever was in the house. That's when I discovered Joey."

A look of horror crossed her face. "He was lying on the floor in the living room. He'd been shot in the head. There was so much blood but I thought he might still be alive. I had to get help right away.

"I was dialing 911 when the police stormed into the house, guns drawn, and scared me out of my wits."

"Wait a minute. How did they get there so fast? Someone had to report the crime. Oh, my gosh, Mel, you were set up."

"You're right. It had to be something like that. And it had to be the killer watching the house, seeing when I went in."

"And he called the news stations too. How else did that television crew get there so quickly? Did you see anyone hanging around when you drove up?" I asked.

"Only the construction crew at the house next door," she replied. "There were carpenters all over the area. So, yes, I did see them and guys in trucks. They were making a terrible racket with their hammers and power saws. Enough noise to cover the gun shots."

"I sure hope the police question them," I said.

"Why should they? They think I did it," she said angrily. "But Walt is hiring a private detective. We'll get to the bottom of this."

"So your fingerprints were on the gun," I prompted.

"Unfortunately so. A Crime Scene technician took my prints and matched them to the prints on the gun. So right away, they assumed I was the murderer. I tried to explain that I'd only touched the gun, that I hadn't fired it, but they wouldn't listen.

"And then — and you won't believe this — remember those two bimbos we saw at Joey's apartment complex on Wednesday."

"Oh, no," I cried.

"Oh, yes," Melanie said. "Those creatures saw me on television so they contacted the police and said I had stolen Joey's car. I told everyone my car was identical to Joey's, that I had not stolen his car, but those guys must have wax in their ears. They just wouldn't listen.

"And they are not even looking for the real killer, that's what makes me so furious. Dear Joey is dead and his killer is getting away, scot free!"

7

Spunky who is not a timid cat and lives up to his name must have been sensing Melanie's mood because he slunk into the bedroom warily. He looked up at us, crouched, then sprang onto the bed. To my astonishment he stepped into my lap.

"Pour us another," Melanie said, holding her empty wine glass aloft.

I settled Spunky in the center of the bed and got up to refill both our glasses.

"Come over here, baby," Melanie told her cat and reached for him. But when I sat back down he again crawled into my lap. The vibes Melanie was giving off had gotten to even him. Spunky was a cat I had rescued as a tiny kitten. But ungrateful beast, one day he had taken a long, hard look into Melanie's kittenish eyes and recognized a kindred spirit. From then on he howled when she left my house. I had no choice but to give him to her.

He is now a fat two year old, black with a white bib and paws, like he's dressed in a tuxedo. He sure lucked out when he met the Wilkes sisters because between us, we treat him like royalty.

Last night, Jon and I had driven to Melanie's house to retrieve Spunky and take him to my house for the night. The three of us settled on the sofa in my library, snuggled for a while, then fell unromantically asleep. The events of the day — finding the skeleton under those bottles, Melanie's arrest, numerous trips from downtown to Wrightsville — had just been too much stress and had worn us out.

At about midnight we awoke. Jon hugged me goodnight and staggered sleepily out the front door, heading for home. Tomorrow was Saturday and we wouldn't be able to work on the hunting lodge, not until Detective Sherwood gave the go ahead. I imagined that Dr. Jamie McAllister and her students would be working all weekend in her lab to solve the mystery of the skeleton we'd found.

Spunky and I had gone upstairs to bed where I struggled with a fit of insomnia. Nick was gone. Even though he had been sleeping in the guest room, the house — and my life — felt empty without him.

Now it was time for me to tell Melanie that Nick had left me. I watched her sip her wine, could see the wheels in her active brain spinning. I stroked Spunky and he purred. They say that petting an animal lowers the blood pressure. I hoped they were right because my life style was setting me up for hypertension.

"Mel, Nick is gone. He left yesterday afternoon. Gone for good," I said mournfully.

She gave me a speculative look, drained her glass, then said, "Good riddance. He never did deserve you."

I told her about the conversation I'd overheard him having with a woman he called Carol, about his admission that there was someone else, about his joining Blackwater Security.

"They are a private army," she said, "and that scares me. They are better equipped and trained than our military. Who can control them? It doesn't really surprise me that Nick would go for that sort of association. He was always rather hawkish."

"Oh, Melanie, but I loved him," I wailed.

"I know you did. But do you now?"

"I don't know anymore."

"I vote for Jon," she said. "He will make you happy. Nick never really made you happy, only needy."

"Maybe you're right but when I was happy with him, I was very, very happy. And I don't like it that *he* rejected *me*."

"No one wants to be the one who gets left," Melanie said. "Mark my words, he'll do the same to this Carol person. Nick answers to the call of a different master."

"What do you mean?" I asked.

"He's an adventurer. He serves the call of adventure. Hearth and home, love, family and kin are not his priorities," she said wisely. "He's a wanderer, likes danger and being on the cutting edge. In ancient days, he'd probably have been an explorer."

"I think I always knew that, Mel. But oh Mel, I also lost my baby. And I don't even know if it was a girl or boy," I cried.

Melanie gave me a level look. "I've been meaning to talk to you about that. Didn't you ever wonder why there's an eight year age gap between us?"

"No," I responded.

"Mama had two miscarriages before you were born. That's why she thought of you as her miracle baby. So none of this is your fault, Ashley Wilkes, and knowing you I suspect you are blaming yourself for losing your baby."

I dropped my head. I had been wondering if I'd done something risky, but censor myself as I had, I couldn't think of a thing. I didn't smoke. I didn't drink caffeinated coffee. I'd given up wine just as soon as I knew I was pregnant and prior to that I'd been drinking only one glass at a time.

Melanie opened her arms to me and I moved into her embrace. "We've got to stick together, little sis. We're the only ones we have. The men will come and go but sisters are forever."

She seemed to brighten, sounded like her old self. "I know what. You and Jon should come out on Cam's yacht with us tomorrow. Give him a call."

8

The first Saturday in November was as warm as June. The sky was clear, the air was balmy, the sea calm. A perfect day for sailing.

Cam's yacht, *Hot Momma*, which he'd purchased last summer when he and Melanie were dating and had named for her, was sleek and trim.

I was so happy to see Cam. He's over six feet tall, lean and rangy, with a boyish face and unruly sandy hair, everybody's favorite big brother. I gave him a hug and whispered conspiratorially that I hoped he was back in Melanie's life for good. He replied that he hoped so too.

Jon presented him with two bottles of champagne. "Hey, Cam, good to see you again," he said and clapped Cam on the back. With his golden blonde good looks, Jon looked spiffy and nautical in white shorts and a navy polo shirt.

We followed Cam onto the flybridge where he settled into one of a pair of brown leather helm chairs.

The view from the flybridge was breathtaking with lush green live oak trees lining the mainland shore on the starboard side and the blue waters of Greenville Sound off the port side.

"Sit over here, Jon," Cam invited, indicating the second helm chair. "Now watch this." Cam slid the throttle forward. "Feel that? No drag. These new boats have a passive tunnel air induction system that virtually eliminates stress. Remember, we're moving 100,000 pounds of fiberglass and iron through the water."

"How does that work?" Jon asked eagerly. "The old boats used to vibrate like mad during acceleration. This one takes off as smooth as silk."

Cam and Jon went on to talk about things like stress and drag, vibration, spiraling low-pressure cavitation voids, wedges, and negative pressure.

Melanie laughed out loud, her effervescent self again, and I hoped it was Cam's influence. "Come on, Ashley, let's go down to the galley, uncork a bottle of bubbly, and I'll tell you about the latest technological breakthrough in panty-hose. There's no drag unless you haven't shaved your legs in days. And they only vibrate if the right man comes danger-ously close."

Cam grinned from ear to ear, we all laughed, and as I fol-lowed Melanie off the bridge, I heard Cam say, "I love that woman."

Jon laughed. "Yeah, and I love the other one. Lord help us, Cam."

We cruised into a cove off Greenville Sound, cut the engines and dropped anchor. Then we gathered in the gal-ley/dining area for lunch. From a full-height refrigerator, Cam withdrew an assortment of sandwiches and salads that the Seventeenth Street Deli at Landfall had prepared for us. I love their salad sampler — tuna, chicken, and egg salad — and went for that. We settled on bar stools around a granite-topped island. And although my salad plate was tasty I was only able to nibble — my appetite had gone the way of my marriage, down the tubes.

Cam's yacht was as luxurious as any finely-appointed home. Three steps down lay the salon, carpeted in pale beige with off-white deeply-upholstered furniture. The paneling and built-ins were made of sleek cherry wood veneers. The headliner was decorated with cherry inlays.

"Are you going to enter your boat in the Holiday Flotilla?" Jon asked Cam.

"Already registered," Cam replied. "Would you like to co-pilot with me?"

"That'd be great," Jon said. "I love the flotilla. Christmas wouldn't be Christmas without the Holiday Flotilla to herald the season."

"And you, Ashley? Will you join us?" Cam asked me. Then beamed at Melanie. "And you, pretty lady?"

Melanie and I looked at each other. "Sure," I said. "Sounds like fun."

"Count me in," Melanie said. "If I'm not in jail."

Cam moved closer to her and put his arm around her shoulders. "Don't even say that. What could those idiots be thinking?"

Melanie rubbed her cheek against his hand.

Cam didn't know what I knew. Melanie had been stalking Joey Fielding. I crossed my fingers under the counter and prayed he'd never find out.

"Let's take this champagne out on the sun deck," Jon proposed. "It's glorious out there."

"These inlets used to make ideal hiding places for pirates," Jon said about the cove where we were docked.

Melanie stretched her legs out into the sun. She had on pale yellow shorts and a matching tee shirt and sun visor. Her bright hair was tied up in a pony tail. "All of my out-of-town clients want to know where Captain Kidd buried his treasure chests," she said. "I tell them Money Island and point it out to them. So many people have been out there digging, the island must look like a sieve. And you know there's no treasure there."

"But it's an important local legend," I said, "part of our heritage. The folklore is that Captain Kidd and his trusted colleague Captain Redfield buried two iron chests filled with gold on Money Island in two deep holes, then planted trees in the holes. Redfield remained behind to guard the treasure while Kidd sailed off. And remember Kidd's treasure has never been found."

"Maybe not just a legend," Jon said. "Researchers are raising cannons from a sunken ship off Atlantic Beach that they believe is Blackbeard's flagship, the *Queen Anne's Revenge.*"

Already the sun was slipping behind the trees. The days are short in November and once the sun goes down the air cools.

"How's the television and film business these days, Cam?" Jon asked. "You guys have been going through a tough time."

"What I don't understand," Melanie complained, "is why they didn't film *Cold Mountain* here since the book was set in our North Carolina mountains? Instead they shot it in some Eastern European country. Yugoslavia, was it?"

"I don't get that either," I said.

"It's the bottom line they're looking at," Cam replied. "A delegation of film and television executives that included Frank Capra Jr. and myself met with the state Senate to seek incentives for the industry, tax breaks that are similar to those offered by other states. The bill passed and I predict better days ahead for us.

"Ashley, have you heard anything more about the skeleton you found at the hunting lodge?"

"Not a word," I replied, "and the place is off limits to us until we get the go ahead, so our restoration project is on hold."

Jon said, "Well, Jamie McAllister left a message for me on my answering machine last night."

"She did?" I asked. Interesting. She had not tried to reach me. I recalled how she had given Jon those hungry female predatory looks. Was she after him? I was starting to see red. Carol after Nick. Jamie after Jon. Over my dead body!

"What did she say?" I asked.

"Just that the body had been there for about eighty years. And she'd keep us posted as she learned more."

Us? Or Jon? I wondered.

Melanie glanced at her watch. "Listen guys, the police notified the Bittermans about the shooting in their house so Bunny and Clay have flown back from Palm Beach. They want to meet us for dinner at Blue Water. I told them we'd join them. And Brie and her manager will be there too. They want to talk to me about what happened.

"And I want you guys to be with me. It's hard enough to rehash finding Joey like that, I don't want to be alone with them. It's all bad news, especially for me, but Bunny and Clay will have a hard time selling that house now, and I expect they want to tell me they are giving the listing to someone else. I can't say I blame them."

Cam put his arms around her. "Rest that pretty head right here, darling. Don't you worry. This will all blow over soon. The police will catch the real killer, and everything will go back to normal."

Melanie gave me a look over Cam's shoulder. Things will never be normal for Joey Fielding, her look said.

9

Darkness had settled in by the time we tied up at the Wrightsville Marina and strolled along the boardwalk to the Blue Water Restaurant. Temperatures that had been in the high eighties during the afternoon had fallen to the mid-seventies, warm enough for outdoor dining even in shorts. The waterway gets incredibly dark at night. The trees were black silhouettes against an aquamarine sky streaked with pink wispy clouds. The water looked inky and opaque, like another world. Like if you dropped into it you'd be gone for good.

I watched my footing.

From the deck we had a clear view of Joey's Place, closed now, locked up tight and totally dark. I wondered what would happen to it.

Palm trees grew on the deck under yellow canvas awnings that were trimmed with rope lights. There were pots of hibiscuses fully blooming with bright red flowers.

The Bittermans were already seated at a large table on the lower deck and Bunny waved when she saw us. Clay stood up.

We all said hello, Jon and Cam were introduced by

Melanie. Brie was silent and sullen, her long hair sheltering most of her face, concealing her identify from other dinner guests. She had on a cropped tank top and wore rings on all her fingers. She looked like any other teenage girl to me, not a mega-star of pop culture.

The man with her, about thirty-five and incredibly homely, stuck out his hand. "Al Shariff," he said. "I'm Brie's manager.

Cam said, "Ali, long time no see." To us, he said, "I know Ali from my HBO days."

Al had thick black hair that stood on end, shaggy brows, hooded piercing black eyes, and stubble on his chin. Swarthy. Middle Eastern.

Bunny Bitterman was in her fifties, petite with very short white-blonde hair, nervous and fidgety and seemed uncomfortable. Clay Bitterman was a big guy who looked like he had downed too many beers and they had all settled in the spare tire around his middle. He had pale hair and watery eyes and a florid complexion. He looked like a bad insurance risk.

"You remember Ashley, don't you?" Melanie asked.

"Yes, of course," Bunny said. "You came with Melanie to our fund raiser for John Edwards." For no apparent reason she giggled. Must be nerves, I figured.

The waiter came up to our table to take our drink orders. The Bitterman crowd had started without us and were ahead in the game. I asked for white wine, and Jon and Cam went for gin and tonics. Melanie, aware that the discussion was going to turn to business, ordered iced tea.

"We thought it would be best if we met somewhere public," Bunny began.

Clay picked up her sentence. "Best not to ask you to the house because of this . . . this mess we find ourselves in."

I could sense what was coming.

For a moment there was an unpleasant silence as the

Bittermans didn't seem to know where to go from there.

At the next table, a woman ignored her dinner companions to talk on her cell phone. "I thought we'd do something different this year," she said loudly. Why do people have to yell into their phones? Like the person on the other end is deaf.

"Not turkey this year," she yelled. "Seafood."

She was planning Thanksgiving dinner.

"How about if we smoke oysters in the backyard?" she asked.

Her voice was grating, like fingernails on a chalkboard. "I said oysters," she shouted. Shut up, already, I wanted to yell at her.

Cam turned to Brie. "Brie, I'd love to give you a show at my studio."

Brie barely lifted her lashes. "You and every other small-time producer," she said with a sneer.

Cam's eyes widened and he looked like he'd been stuck. He was such a gentle soul to have him spoken to like that was insulting. I glared at her but she seemed not to notice. She was miles away.

One thing I can say for Melanie though is that she is a very classy lady. "Bunny, Clay, Brie, I can see this is really hard for you. I know what you must be going through. Your house was a crime scene. I can't tell you how terrible it was for me, finding Joey that way. And now, well, with the way the police are focusing on me — unjustly I might add — I'll understand if you are thinking of going with another broker. I can recommend one of my associates. She'll do a bang-up job for you. Not as good as me," Melanie chuckled like a good sport, "but she's very experienced."

"You don't understand anything," Clay snapped.

Bunny's nervous fingers shredded a dinner roll to crumbs. "Melanie, it's just that . . ."

"We can't sell the damned house now," Clay said angrily. "No one will buy a house where there's been a murder." He turned and stared out at the water, as if his rage could turn the tide.

"We've decided to take it off the market for a while," said Bunny the peacemaker, not wanting to upset anyone. "Just until the fuss dies down, Melanie. You understand."

Clay glared at Melanie. "And then you can bet your boots, young lady, you will not get the listing."

"Now, wait a . . . " Cam started to say in Melanie's defense.

Brie, whose sullen attitude caused her to appear morose, leaned forward so that her face was inches from Melanie's. I had seen her on MTV and major network shows. She was the hottest new star in the music world. When I'd seen her on TV, she'd been all over the stage, trotting back and forth, prancing, dancing, tossing her long mane, the mike in her hand, singing her heart out. How could any one person possess so much energy? Perhaps because she was only seventeen?

Now all of that energy was fixed on Melanie. "I want to know," she shouted, "why you shot my fiance?"

"Your . . . what?" Melanie stammered.

Fiance? And that explained something that had been puzzling me, namely, why had Joey Fielding been in the Bitterman house that day? Now I wondered if he had been there to meet Brie.

Brie was on her feet. "My fiance," she shouted. "Joey Fielding. The man I loved. The man who loved me. The man I was going to marry and spend my life with. Have babies with. Why did you kill him?"

The restaurant deck went silent. Everyone stopped talking, listened and stared. And they recognized Brie. In a second she was going to be mobbed.

I placed my hand firmly on Melanie's thigh. As if to

ground her, to hold her down. I increased the pressure of my hand, silently telling her to be careful what she said. To not make a fool of herself.

I could see the control she was exerting over her emotions. "Brie," she said in a reasonable voice, "Joey was my friend. I did not kill him."

Tears in her eyes, Brie protested, "During the summer, when I was on my Australian tour, you were there, always hanging around him. Every time I called you were there!"

"Well, of course, I was there," Melanie said soothingly. "I was his realtor. I found him that fabulous location for his restaurant." She pointed toward Joey's Place with her hand.

"And Brie, he talked about you constantly. He told me all about the engagement and your wedding plans."

I could see what those words cost Melanie, but no one else could. No one knew her the way I did.

For a second Brie seemed unsure of what to say next. "I'm getting out of here," she cried. "Come on, Ali." She turned on her stilettos and marched up the stairs.

Al Shariff stood up, his angry, piercing eyes glaring at Melanie. "She can't work. She can't sing. She's cancelled her London tour. This is costing her a bundle. And it's all your fault."

"Wait a minute," Cam yelled. "You can't talk to her like that."

"Yeah," Jon said. "What don't we all cool off."

"Cool off! Do you have any idea what she has to pay in fines when she cancels a tour?" He stomped off after Brie.

Bunny jumped up. "Brie! Brie, honey, wait for mommy." And she was off too.

With that, Clay pushed away from the table. "Keep away from my family," he growled at Melanie, and started to go.

I stood up. "Just a minute here," I declared, "you're the one who scheduled this cozy little get-together!"

Clay lumbered off, huffing and puffing as he climbed the stairs.

Melanie buried her face in her hands. Her shoulders were shaking. But when she uncovered her face, I saw she was laughing.

"This is not my life," she blurted. "Someone has stolen my life and replaced it with this nightmare."

"Okay, baby, we're going to leave now," Cam said and got up, taking Melanie's arm.

Jon stood up too and threw some money on the table. "Cheapskate stiffed us for his drinks," he said resentfully.

"This is a nightmare," Melanie repeated. "What else can go wrong?"

Two people were approaching our table. "Oh, no, not them. Not now," I breathed.

10

"Were those the Bittermans we just missed?" David Boleyn asked. "Too bad. Clay and I go way back. Now, what's this I hear about you folks? A friend called me and gave me an earful about what's been going on here while we were out at sea," he continued. "We sailed back to shore as quickly as the boat could get us here."

The "boat" that David Boleyn referred to was an eighty foot yacht named the *Crystal Lynne.*

Mrs. Crystal Lynne Boleyn was at his side, a Dolly Parton look-alike with flowing platinum blonde hair and implants so big they cleared a path for her. Melanie had clued me in about the breast implants. I need clues about such matters because the truth is I don't have a clue. I just thought Mother Nature had been generous to Crystal Lynne.

Melanie and Crystal embraced and kissed the air at each other's cheeks. "Crystal used to be my dearest friend," Melanie told us, "in our pageant days. How are you, sweetie?"

Crystal said she was fine as David pulled out a chair for her.

Over the years, Melanie had told me the sordid details of

Crystal's unsuccessful marriages — the infidelities, the legal battles. "This time she landed a big fish," Melanie had said.

David took the chair that Clay Bitterman had vacated and settled into it.

Jon shook hands and said something like "nice to see you again" to our client and his wife.

Cam stretched a hand across the table and introduced himself. "It's a pleasure to meet you, David. I've heard a lot about you."

Prior to David's recent retirement he had been a consultant to and a representative of the tobacco industry. In other words, a lobbyist. He directed huge contributions to favorite politicians. He dined with senators and cabinet members. He was a Washington insider, a mover and a shaker. He still dabbled in his chosen field, he had told us, maintained close ties with the rulers of the world — his words.

David and Crystal lived aboard a yacht while we worked to restore his grandfather's hunting lodge that David had recently taken an interest in. They sailed from Miami to Boston and back again, with frequent layovers at the Wrightsville Marina while David checked our progress on the lodge.

"So what is this nonsense about finding some old bones under a pile of rubbish?" David asked bruskly. David could turn on the charm when he chose. He did not choose now, did not seem to think any of us at the table merited the effort.

Jon and I explained how we'd found a skeleton in a shed.

"The body has been buried there for about eighty years," Jon said.

"Probably an animal," David said.

"Oh, it's a human," I said. "A forensic anthropologist from the university exhumed the bones and says they are human."

David stared me down. "I know all about the forensic

anthropologist. And when that little girl gets her act together, she'll see it was just some large animal."

There was no arguing with David. And he'd never admit he was wrong. The truth was my client intimidated me.

Melanie was watching him over the rim of her iced tea glass with one of her narrow eyed, I've got you in the crosshairs expressions. She had never met him before. What must she think of him?

David turned to her. "And I saw you on the TV news too, little lady. They keep rerunning that shot of you in handcuffs. You gals sure have a way of turning up the volume. Can't you fellows keep these girls in line?" he asked Cam and Jon.

Jon choked on his gin and tonic. I knew what he was thinking. Keep Ashley in line? Are you crazy? And Melanie's even worse.

Cam interjected, "It's all a big misunderstanding, David, and the police will soon see that it is."

"David, honey, I'm hungry," Crystal whined. "And thirsty. Get the waiter over here and order me a drink."

David gave her a look but said nothing. He snapped his fingers in the air and darn if a waiter didn't come trotting up to the table.

Crystal ordered chardonnay and the seafood sampler.

"Would you like that fried or broiled?" the waiter asked.

"Broiled," she replied. "I've got to watch my figure."

David grinned. "Don't you worry none, honey, there's plenty of us doing that for you."

"Mr. Boleyn, the . . . ," I said.

"Now Ashley, how many times do I have to tell you? Mr. Boleyn was my daddy. I'm David," he said.

"David," I repeated. "David, we're hoping to get back to work on Monday. The police have sealed the property while they do their investigating about the remains we found."

"Bring me a Jack Daniels straight up," David told the waiter. "And a steak, New York strip. Rare."

Dismissing the waiter and turning to me, he said, "You can get back to work first thing tomorrow. The North Carolina Attorney General is a close personal friend of mine. He put in a call to that viper-tongued detective and set her straight. No excuse not to work. No one will stop you and your workers from returning to my property."

Absently David patted his shirt pocket, withdrawing a pack of Camels and a gold cigarette lighter. He put a cigarette in his mouth, lit it, inhaled, placed the gold lighter on the table and regarded it fondly.

"A present from old Jesse," he said as he exhaled, blowing a stream of smoke across the table.

Jesse? Of course, Jesse Helms, the former senator.

I coughed. Melanie fanned the air in front of her face.

"You got a problem with cigarettes?" David confronted her.

Melanie had taken as much as she was going to take. I knew the signs and she was about to explode. Watch out!

She leaned forward and glared at him. "No North Carolina family as old as mine has a problem with cigarettes. Why, the tobacco crop built this state and fine institutions like Duke University with their huge medical/research complex. The tobacco companies provided good paying jobs for our workers when there were no others. And the tobacco companies give back to the community. No other industry donates as much to local worthwhile causes as the tobacco companies. And their employees organize to do volunteer work like building houses for Habitat for Humanity.

"So, no Mr. Boleyn, I do not have a problem with cigarettes! But I do have a problem with smokers who blow smoke in my face. I also have a problem with smokers who drop cigarette butts all over the sidewalks of my lovely city."

Boleyn stuck his cigarette between his lips and with his

free hands applauded. "If I wasn't retired I'd offer you a job in my Washington office on K Street," he said.

Melanie smiled smugly. "You couldn't afford me."

David regarded her through squinted eyes but he took care to direct his smoke off to the water side of the table. Had the omnipotent David Boleyn finally met his match?

"As I was saying," David continued then as if Melanie had not spoken, "tobacco lost a good friend when Jesse retired. Now look at what's happening to our industry. The DOJ is breathing down our necks, trying to put us out of business. Everyone thought the Bush administration would look favorably on big tobacco, but no-sirree-bob, they're panting after us just as hot and heavy as the Clintons.

"They seem to forget that tobacco is a legal product. If they spent half as much money on going after illegal drugs the way they spend it on persecuting the tobacco industry, there wouldn't be any more crack babies born up there in Harlem."

Was there no group David did not regard with prejudice?

Melanie's eyes were shooting daggers at me. I'd hear about this later. Cam was getting an edgy look and shifted in his chair. Jon's face had grown progressively red. Crystal Lynne took solace in her wine glass, no doubt having these tirades all too many times.

I started to stand up. "We're meeting someone for dinner," I said. "We've got to get going. We'll . . . "

But David had not finished delivering his tirade.

"The federal government taxes cigarettes through the manufacturers. The states tax cigarettes at point of sale. North Carolina's got it right. Five cents a pack. But up there in Taxachusets, they levy an excise tax of one dollar fifty-one cents on a single pack. And folks have got to go out and stand on the sidewalks to smoke.

"New York is just as bad. Buck fifty. Then New York City has got a municipal tax of another buck fifty, so they pay three dollars on the pack. Maine, Michigan two dollars a pack. But the one that beats all is little Rhode Island. Two dollars and forty six cents tax on twenty cigarettes. No wonder they cost so much. Folks don't need none of them patches to quit smoking. They simply can't afford to pay the price. Then we've got the FDA breathing down our necks, wanting to control our product."

David was fuming, had worked himself into a fever pitch. He shook a fresh cigarette out the pack, put it in his mouth, and lit it from the glowing butt end of the one he held in his hand. Then he took a deep drag.

The nicotine seemed to calm him for he then surprised me by smiling broadly. "Now to get to the real reason we're here," he said. "Crystal and I spent our honeymoon at Borgo Lucchese."

He paused long enough to leer at her. What an obnoxious man, I thought.

"It's a lavish estate in Tuscany near Lucca. We want you to do more than restore my granddaddy's lodge to its original condition, we want you to make it as beautiful as Borgo Lucchese. Think you're up to that?" he demanded.

"Of course we can," Jon assured him. "They must have a website. I'll download the site, see what we can learn from that."

"Forget about the internet stuff," David said as he intercepted his drink from the waiter. "I want you to eyeball Borgo Lucchese up close and personal. You're leaving for Italy on Tuesday. Tickets, everything all arranged. You go over there, spend a few days, take pictures, talk to the folks, then you come back here and create me a replica. But don't bother with the furnishings or the decorating. Crystal is a good little decorator and wants to do that part herself."

I was almost speechless. "Italy? Tuesday?"

David glared at me. "You got a problem with that, little girl?"

Melanie could not restrain her temper a minute longer. "Is every woman a little girl to you?" she demanded, pushing back her chair and standing up.

David's eyes danced merrily. He had gotten to her again. His intention.

"You got a fire in your belly, little lady," he said. "I like that in a woman. But no, ma'am, to answer your question, some of them are big girls."

I swallowed and said, "No problem with going to Italy."

Jon got up, did not bother to shake hands. He was seething. "You can decorate that lodge anyway you like. Early whorehouse if that's your style. But that lodge was designed to look like it was Italian and four hundred years old and that is how we're going to restore it."

David did not take offense. He reared back and roared with laughter. What a strange man.

"Our reputations are on the line. We've worked hard to make a name for ourselves as restorers, and one man's whimsy is not going to compromise that. Feel free to find yourself another restoration firm if you want to."

I was so proud of Jon I could have kissed him.

"Fair enough," the mercurial David said. "Then you're off to Italy. Think of it as a romantic holiday with a pretty lady. On me. Maybe you'll get lucky, like I did."

11

"And I thought my clients were bad," Melanie said as we walked her and Cam to the boat.

"Ashley and I have had our share of nutty clients," Jon said. "But we've survived them and come out on top. Increase Boleyn's hunting lodge is an architectural treasure, important to the area."

"Was his first name actually Increase?" Cam asked as he headed up the gangplank.

"It really was," I said. "He was David's grandfather. A successful banker until the stock market crash in 1929. He built the hunting lodge in 1899."

I continued, "A speculator had bought it from David's aunt for a song back in the sixties and was just holding on to it. David bought it back in the seventies when he was making a lot of money. In fact, he rescued it in the nick of time but paid dearly for land that ought to have been his birthright. The lodge was about to be torn down and the land developed. Then he lost interest and place just sat there deteriorating until just recently. Guess he was waiting to retire before doing something about it."

"He sure is a funny guy," Cam said.

"Funny?" Melanie declared. "He's certifiable."

"Well, none of us have had time for dinner," Cam said. "Why don't I go back to the restaurant and pick up some take out? We can eat on the boat."

"That terrible man cost me my appetite," Melanie said.

"Me too," I said. "I'll have a bowl of cereal or something when I get home."

"Listen, shug, I'm going to spend the night on the boat with Cam. Would you stop at my house and pick up Spunky and take him home with you for the rest of the weekend?"

"Sure, I'll be glad to."

I kissed them goodnight and Jon and I headed down the gangplank, crossed over the boardwalk, and walked to our cars in the parking lot.

"Sure you don't want to go out for a bite to eat?" Jon asked as I clicked the remote and unlocked my car door. He sounded almost shy. The transition from best friends to potential lovers was making both of us a bit giddy. We were on unfamiliar ground.

I looked into his face and smiled, brushing back a lock of blond hair that fallen onto his forehead. "I'm as beat as Melanie is. David Boleyn did me in too. I just want to go home and crash. I'll meet you at the site early tomorrow morning."

He buzzed me on the cheek. "Drive carefully."

I drove over the bridge to the mainland in full darkness. It was only eight o'clock but felt much later. I turned left onto Airlie Road and followed the waterway. Across Motts Channel, the Blue Water Restaurant was lit up like a Mississippi show-boat, but a few doors down Joey's Place was closed up tight and shrouded in darkness.

Turning inland I passed the narrow driveway that led to Increase Boleyn's hunting lodge. Bright light cast by a channel marker out in the water backlit the crenelated tower that rose above the tree line. Jon was right. The hunting lodge was architecturally significant, an important landmark to the area. I would put up with the eccentric David Boleyn for the privilege of restoring his lodge.

Next I passed Bradley Creek Road on my left, then the entrance to Airlie Gardens where, at about the same time that Increase Boleyn had entertained at his hunting lodge, Sarah and Pembroke Jones had entertained at their mansion. There were stories about the lavish parties the Joneses had given, of private railway cars for their New York and Newport guests. The Great Caruso himself had been a guest and had entertained for Mrs. Jones. One tale in particular stood out: elegant dinner parties held on specially built platforms in live oak trees, complete with musicians and spiraling staircases.

At the intersection, I turned left onto Oleander Drive for the short hop to Bradley Creek and across the bridge. I then made a sharp left into the heavily wooded neighborhood at Greenville Loop Road. Melanie lived at the end of Sandpiper Cove off Rabbit Run in a rambling ranch with bleached cedar shakes, green shutters, and a split rail fence covered with late-blooming rambling roses. Her backyard overlooked Hewlett's Creek and Greenville Sound and she had a private boat dock.

My headlights picked out the opening in the fence and I maneuvered my car down her sloping, sandy driveway.

I drive a white van for work with our logo imprinted on the side, the outline of a Greek Revival house, and our company name, Wilkes Campbell Restorations. My own car is a pale blue Toyota Avalon, very pretty, and if a car could be described as feminine, then my car was feminine.

Melanie's porch light was on, plus a few lights inside, and solar lights lined the walkway to her porch. I removed her front door key from my purse, left the purse on the passenger seat, and locked my car with a click of the remote.

I unlocked the front door and stepped inside, expecting Spunky to come running to meet me, to feel his furry body warp around my ankles and hear him meowing loudly. Spunky is a sociable cat and does not like to be left alone. But he did not appear. I hoped he wasn't hiding because cats can hide good.

As I walked down the hall calling for him, I heard the sound of running water. Alarmed, I followed the sound to the hall bathroom. Had one of the pipes sprung a leak? Did Melanie forget to turn off the faucet?

The door to the bathroom stood ajar and steam plumed around it. The shower? The shower was running.

The bathroom door squeaked on its hinges as I pushed it fully open. From inside the steam shrouded glass shower, a man's voice called, "Hey, babe, you back? Come on in here and join me."

The glass door swung open and a very wet, very naked man greeted me with a smile.

Mickey Ballantine!

His black body hair was soaked and matted flat against his chest. Water dripped from the black hair on his head.

Seeing me, he laughed, "Ooops," and yanked the door closed.

I tossed a towel over the top of the shower door. "Turn that water off, get dry and dressed, and come out. You've got some explaining to do!"

I marched self-righteously into the kitchen and removed a wine bottle from Melanie's wine fridge. I popped the cork and filled a large glass.

I was furious. First David Boleyn, then Mickey Ballantine. Some men! What was he doing here? How had he gotten in? Melanie couldn't know that he was here or she wouldn't have sent me to collect Spunky. She knew how I felt about Mickey Ballantine. But at some point she must have given him a key. *Oh, Melanie, you do enjoy courting danger.*

"She is already in enough trouble without you putting her at risk!" I declared when Mickey made an appearance in the living room. He was wearing a dark suit, dark shirt opened at the throat. He dropped a duffel bag on the carpeting with a soft thud.

"It's not what you think, Ashley," he countered.

"How do you know what I think?" I demanded, standing up to confront him. "I think you're mooching off her. You're running from the law and you're sneaking in here and laying low when you get the chance and taking advantage of her generosity. In case you haven't heard, she's been charged with murder, and if the police find out she's hiding you, things will go even harder for her."

"Murder!" Mickey said contemptuously. "And what's that all about? Them cops don't know nothing. Melanie wouldn't waste a bullet on a lightweight like Fielding." He grinned. "She might blow a hole in a guy like me, but Fielding? Forget it."

It was clear that Mickey did not know that Melanie had been stalking Joey Fielding. That she had been obsessed with him. And that she had been having an affair with Joey at the same time she'd been involved with Mickey. If he had known, Mickey Ballantine would be number one on my list of suspects who might have killed Joey. And I did not want him to know. There was no telling what a loose cannon like Mickey would do if he found out he'd been double crossed.

"How do you know I haven't called the cops on you?" I said. "How do you know they aren't on their way here right now?"

He laughed tauntingly. "Because, Ashley, you're a nice little girl. You'd never do that. Besides you owe me."

There was that phrase again. Little girl. What was it with

some men? Men were men, but women were not women, but girls. Little girls.

Still I had steered him off the subject of Joey Fielding.

"Okay, Ashley, let me explain how it is. Melanie and me, we don't have a romantic thing going for us anymore. But we're friends. And Melanie, when she's your friend, she's loyal."

That was true. If Melanie was your friend, she'd do anything for you.

"So she lets me crash here now and then. My nightclub has been closed by the police. The owner has 'For Lease' signs plastered all over it. So I have to stay on the move. Can't settle in one place for too long. Melanie lets me spend a few hours here when I don't have no place else to go. I keep a few things here. I come in when she's not at home, when it's quiet around the neighborhood, take a nap. Grab a sandwich. Shower, change. Then I'm on my way again."

I shook my head. "Mickey, why don't you just leave town? Go back to Atlantic City? You've got family there. Friends. Wouldn't it be easier to allude that warrant on your own turf?"

"Can't leave right now, Ashley. I've got a deal going here. Somebody owes me a lot of money. When I collect, I'm out of here."

"And you're out of here right now," I said and stretched out my palm. "The key. Now."

He dug into a pocket and produced a key, dropped it in my palm. Then he reached down, picked up the duffel bag, and walked past me. At the sliding glass door, he turned, "So long, Ashley."

He unlatched the door, slid it open, and stepped out into the darkness.

I moved to the door and looked for him. I almost didn't see him. A faint shadow moved down the lawn to the boat dock. So that was why I hadn't seen a car in the driveway or parked in the street near the house. Mickey was living on a boat, a small boat.

Distantly, I heard the motor start, then saw a dark shape sail out into the sound. And Mickey Ballantine was gone. I hoped he would not enter our lives again.

12

I locked the glass door and drew the curtains. I dropped the key in the fruit bowl on the kitchen counter. Then I poured myself another glass of wine, searched around, found some cheese and crackers, and had just popped one in my mouth when Spunky slunk into the kitchen, hair all spiky, looking around suspiciously.

"It's okay," I said, "he's gone."

Spunky hates Mickey, and with good reason.

I broke off a bit of cheese and held it out to him. He licked it off my finger with his scratchy tongue. Then he gave me a long, unblinking cat look.

"Hungry?" I asked.

In answer, he sat down and wrapped his tail around his haunches, and stared at the upper cabinet where Melanie keeps his Fancy Feast. He ate his tuna delicately; I made a mess of the cheese and crackers. I placed our dirty dishes in the dishwasher, brushed up the crumbs, and was on my way to get his pet carrier from the hall closet when the doorbell rang.

Oh, no, not Mickey again. I yanked the door open and took a deep breath, ready to blast him.

The man standing under the porch light was not Mickey. I had never seen him before. I pushed the door closed immediately, put the chain on, then opened it a crack. My watch cat had vanished.

"Yes?" I said through the crack.

"I'm looking for Ashley Wilkes," the man said. He was not friendly nor unfriendly, just determined.

"Who are you and what do you want?"

"Are you Ashley Wilkes?" he asked. "I tried the house on Nun Street but she . . . you . . . were not there. If you're Ashley I've got to speak to you."

"You still haven't told me who you are," I said, about ready to slam the door shut on him.

"My name is Scott Randolph and I'm an agent with ATF, that's Alcohol, Tobacco, and Firearms. Here's my ID."

He stuck a plasticized photo ID and a heavy metal shield in a leather case through the crack in the door. I held up the photo. It was him all right. I moved the shield to the light. It looked official to me but what do I know?

I handed his ID back to him. "You can probably buy that shield on the internet."

I'd meant it as a joke but he did not laugh. Instead he growled, "Not this shield."

From what little I could see of him through the crack in the door, he was tall and big, probably muscular if he was really an agent. He had dark brown eyes, dark brown hair, a square jaw. He looked like a hundred other men.

"Okay," I said, "I'll accept that you are who you say you are. What do you want?"

"I'd like to come in," he said firmly.

"Let someone in my house I've never seen before just because he has a tin badge? No way." What I was thinking was that he was after Mickey Ballantine. That whatever deal Mickey was involved in was of interest to the ATF. And I wondered if Mickey had left something incriminating behind. And would Melanie be implicated?

"Then step out here. We'll talk on the porch."

"That's not smart either. We'll talk this way, through the door. What do you want with me?"

He shrugged, controlling his anger. "So you are Ashley Wilkes. Okay. As I said, I'm Agent Scott Randolph. I work out of the Charlotte Field Office and I'm working a case in this area. Official ATF business. Then we learned that you had discovered the remains of a man who is of interest to our agency. I was assigned that case as well. We have reason to believe the man you discovered had been one of our agents, an agent who went missing seventy-five years ago."

"Oh," I said softly. I unchained the door and opened it. "Come in."

I led him into the living room. "Would you like something to drink? Tea? Water?" I offered as he sat down in a comfy club chair.

"Nothing, thanks. I'd like you to tell me about how you found those remains, and I'd like to arrange to see where you found them."

"Why aren't you working with the police? They could show you the shed," I said. I still wasn't sure this man was who he said he was.

"How I work my cases is none of your concern. We can't always involve the locals in what we're doing. Not since 9/11. Everything changed then, as I'm sure you know." He came across as dour as J. Edgar Hoover.

"Okay," I said and sat down across from him, clasped my hands in my lap and began the story of first finding the bottles, of contacting the Raleigh Bottle Club members and their arrival, of seeing the outline of a face under the broken glass.

Agent Randolph nodded. "Tell me what you know about the history of the property."

I told him about Increase Boleyn, how he'd been a successful banker in Wilmington, with a house downtown, and the hunting lodge on the water. How he'd lost just about everything in the great stock market crash. "He died right before World War II. His children inherited the lodge and lived there. His only son, David Boleyn, Sr., died in the war. Then a daughter died.

"The surviving daughter married, then in the sixties she sold the land to a speculator. Eventually, our client, Increase Boleyn's grandson, acquired his family's land. The property has come full circle, back to the Boleyn family, and my partner and I are restoring the lodge for Mr. Boleyn."

Scott leaned forward earnestly. "We know who David Boleyn is."

"Well, I'm trying to be helpful," I said. "The remains were taken to the university to Dr. McAllister's lab. Perhaps you should contact her. Or is she one of the locals you have to avoid?"

Randolph did not look happy with my attempt at sarcasm. "I've already spoken to her. Okay, I'll tell you what I can. The Bureau of Alcohol, Tobacco, Firearms and Explosives is a bureau of the Department of Treasury. It's an outgrowth of the old Revenue Department. During the Twenties and Thirties in the Prohibition Era, the agents were called Revenuers or Revenue Men.

"Oh, I know. Around North Carolina and Georgia, the Revenue men were the villains and the moonshiners were the heroes. But that's just myth, Miss Wilkes." He gave me a grim look. "Folklore."

"I don't know much about the subject," I admitted. "Never interested, I guess. My dad was a Superior Court judge. He wouldn't have glamorized people who broke the law."

"I know who your dad was," he said curtly.

I suspected he had checked me out. Had checked Daddy out too. He would have discovered that my dad's reputation was sterling.

He would have also learned that Melanie had been charged with murder and that her reputation was tarnished.

He continued, "There was nothing romantic about moonshining. Most of the moonshiners were to be pitied. They were mostly poor and illiterate. They had no profession, no training. So they did the only thing they knew how to do: made whiskey. They had no respect for the law. In fact they were a law unto themselves. They lived in small enclaves back in the hills, or here on the coast, they lived deep in the wooded swampy areas, apart from society.

"Making moonshine was hard work. They needed all the free labor they could get so they didn't send their kids to school, they put them to work stirring those vats — hogsheads they were called — and their pregnant wives too. It was a rough life. Nothing glamorous or romantic about it. Do you know that it took seven to ten gallons of mash to yield one gallon of whiskey?"

"I didn't know that," I said. "Not a very good yield."

He went on. "And those stills were made of copper. Copper corrodes. At high temperatures, it oxidizes. If they weren't kept clean, the copper would leach into the whiskey. Often the whiskey they made was poisonous, and it killed people. They killed people. And for what? A few pennies."

"I had no idea," I said.

"And then there were the wars. The agents would get a lead, go after a still to close it down, and end up getting shot at. End up dead.

"In 1924, a police officer and a US Marshal were ambushed in their car on a lonely road in the Brunswick Swamps. They were leaving the scene, driving back toward town, but the moonshiners shot them to death anyway. Even killed their pet dog, an Airedale."

"No!" I exclaimed. I abhor cruelty to animals.

"I'd like to meet you tomorrow morning on the Boleyn property, take a look around for myself. As I said, in 1931 a Revenue agent disappeared in this area. If those remains you found are his, we'd like to know. And if we can find out how he died, that would be better. He was one of ours. And our agency takes care of its own."

13

Agent Randolph met Jon and me at the Boleyn property on Sunday morning. The sun was shining, the air was invigorating, another beautiful day shaping up.

The shed had been cordoned off with crime scene tape but there was no need to cross the line. The doors of the shed were propped open and we had an unobstructed view of the interior. The glass shards and earth that had served as the dead man's grave for almost a century had been removed. I speculated that at her lab Dr. McAllister had assigned students to sift through the glass and earth to look for clues.

We strolled down the lane toward the water and the boat dock. Agent Randolph had been silent but when he saw the boat dock, he said, "This dock is fairly new."

"Yes," I said, "David Boleyn had it rebuilt about a year ago before he hired us to restore the lodge. He wanted to have a dock here so he could visit his property whenever he wished." I told the agent how David and Crystal Boleyn lived on their yacht. "There are lots of people who live on yachts: 'live-aboard boaters,' they're called.

"The Boleyns berth at the Wrightsville Marina when

they're in this area. The marina offers wetslips, power, water and fuel."

Randolph stared across Motts Channel. Whatever he was thinking, he kept to himself. A man who kept his own counsel.

To me the view was inspiring and healing at the same time. I could only admire it and feel deeply contented. The colorful cottages on Harbor Island and Wrightsville Beach seemed to be dozing in the warm sun. The water looked peaceful, yet in places was deceptively swift.

"Is it always this quiet out here on a Sunday morning?" Randolph asked.

"Yes," Jon replied. "Willie Hudson, our general contractor, is a Southern Baptist and does not work on Sunday. And the Italian craftsmen who are doing some specialty work for us are Catholic and feel the same. Suits us. We all need a day of rest. Ashley and I become so intense about whatever project we're working on, we tend to go full throttle 24/7."

Scott looked from Jon to me and I could see he was trying to calculate just how much of a couple we really were.

"How long have you been working together?" he inquired.

"Two years," I replied. "My first job was the restoration of the Campbell House on Orange Street. Jon was the architect on the project. Reggie Campbell was a distant relative of Jon's. Then Jon helped me to restore my own house on Nun Street, a rush job because the house had to be completed in time for the annual Candlelight Tour that year."

"We've been partners ever since," Jon said. "Where are you from, Agent Randolph?"

"Atlanta. The men in my family have worked for the Treasury Department since about 1900. My own father was one of the ATF agents who cracked the last big illegal distillery in Georgia in the sixties. Guy had a twenty foot boiler and

54 fermenters that held 220 gallons each. The agents blew it up, put him out of business." Agent Randolph smiled for the first time.

"I thought moonshining was something they did during Prohibition, I didn't know they were making moonshine in the sixties," I said. "Did you, Jon?"

Jon said no.

Randolph looked at us like we were ignorant. "Most people don't know any better. Did you know there's been moonshining going on in this country since Colonial days? Early colonists were the first bootleggers, smuggling whiskey to the Indians by hiding flasks in their boots, then pulling their pant leg down over the boot."

"Hmmm," I said, thinking that was a cute story I'd have to remember. Agent Randolph would not have taken kindly to my thinking his story was cute. He was a deadly serious fellow.

Randolph continued, "The fact is the government has always levied a high tax on whiskey and tobacco and a lot of folks resent paying the tax. The first Whiskey Rebellion broke out in 1794. But with the onset of the Civil War the government re-imposed excise taxes to help pay for the war. Taxes have only increased since then. Whiskey is considered a luxury, not a necessity."

This guy was as much fun as a broken leg. "Oh, I don't know about that, Agent Randolph. At the end of some days, a drink is an absolute necessity for me," I said, trying to lighten the mood.

"I don't drink myself," he said, deadpan.

I turned to Jon. "Agent Randolph thinks the man we found might have been a revenue agent working here during Prohibition."

"Is that right?" Jon asked. "And you think he was murdered by a moonshiner who was operating a still on this property? The representative of the Raleigh Bottle Club swears that the bottles and jars we found in the shed had been used for sour mash liquor. Said they had a distinctive odor."

"Sour mash does have a distinct smell that once you're familiar with it you can detect," Randolph said. "Didn't you say that Increase Boleyn owned this land in 1931?"

"According to the tax records he did," I said. "Boleyn acquired this parcel of land in 1890. At the time there was a small hotel and some cottages out here that were later acquired by Pembroke Jones when he formed the Sea Side Park Development company. Jones bought up land around Bradley Creek to develop into a resort. This area was connected to Wilmington by the Seashore Railroad then later the Beach Trolley."

Randolph looked around and nodded. "Go on," he said.

"I'm not boring you with this local history stuff?" I asked.

"Knowledge is power, Miss Wilkes. You know that."

Jon stared at him as if he was an alien species. I too did not know what to make of him.

"Well, okay, then. Sarah Green bought 52 acres and continued to buy up land piecemeal until she had created the 150 acre Airlie estate, now Airlie Gardens. Sarah Green and Pembroke Jones got married. Their land holdings and wealth were legendary. They built a mansion at Airlie that had 38 apartments and twelve bedrooms, with a covered tennis court right in the middle of the house. Very lavish.

"Jones acquired Pembroke Park, north of here on the other side of Eastwood Road on Wrightsville Sound, fenced it as a hunting preserve, and built an Italian villa-style hunting lodge for himself and his buddies. Seemed to be the thing that rich gentlemen did in those days. That area is now the Landfall development. It's called Landfall because that is where Giovanni da Verrazano made his first landfall in America in 1524.

"Probably the Joneses wanted to acquire this little peninsula too, but Boleyn held onto it. Jones died in 1919 and Sarah already had established her Airlie Gardens."

Jon said, "Probably after the stock market crash, Boleyn resorted to making moonshine here. Seems logical to me. Who else would have put those bottles in that shed?"

"You don't think Boleyn killed your agent, do you?" I asked Agent Randolph.

"Somebody did. He didn't bury himself in that ground in that shed. It's an old crime, and the killer will be dead by now, but there is closure to be had. My agency doesn't like unsolved mysteries where our agents are concerned, no matter how old the crime."

"You said yesterday that when those local agents were shot, their dog was shot too. It really upsets me that anyone would shoot an innocent dog. But why did the agents take a cute little Airedale with them when they were out hunting for stills?"

"Don't know. Could have been for the company. Or the animal might have been a working dog. Might have been trained to smell the mash and help the agents locate the still."

"Oh, like our modern K9 units," I said. And that reminded me of Nick's new girlfriend who was a trainer of K9 units, and that thought made me depressed.

I turned away from them and averted my face. Looking across the marshes at the scenic view, I couldn't help wondering what Carol had that I did not. What was she offering Nick that I didn't have to give? The thought that he preferred another woman to me made me question my own femininity, my womanhood. I didn't like the feeling.

I started to walk back toward the lodge; the men trailed along behind. Agent Randolph was doing the talking. Was he warming up to us?

"The odd thing is that before Prohibition," he said,

"North Carolina produced more wine than any other state. The Scuppernong grapes here were extraordinarily plentiful. Then the state passed Prohibition in 1909, ten years before the nation went dry. From 1909 till 1935, there was so much illegal whiskey dumped in the Cape Fear River, why the fish must have been on a perpetual high."

Jon laughed.

I frowned. I too had been dumped. And I didn't like the feeling, not one bit. Resentment was setting in, an ugly feeling, making me feel mean. "Blast you Nick," I swore under my breath.

Behind me Jon said, "You said you were here on an official case. What case are you working on?"

"I'm not at liberty to discuss that," Randolph replied curtly.

After that we walked him to the lodge in silence.

The structure was in ruins, having been abandoned to the elements for decades. It was a miracle it had not burned. The bones were good, classically Italianate with a low-pitched roof, wide eaves, portico, a few surviving balustrades. Willie and his crew had been removing the crumbling intonaco, a stucco-like material, and repairing the brick substructure. New stucco would be applied.

Inside there were solid chestnut beams in the great hall, two massive fireplaces, one at each end of the thirty foot hall. Under dirt and rubbish, we had discovered a tile and terrazzo floor. Italian craftsmen had been hired to restore the floor but their first job was repairs to the tile roof.

The agent gave us a brusk thank you and drove off.

"He's not talking," Jon said.

"I think he's working on something that has to do with Mickey Ballantine," I said, and told him about my encounter with Ballantine at Melanie's house yesterday.

Jon shook his head. "Ashley, what does Melanie do, put

an ad in the personals asking for scumbags?"

"It does seem that way," I said. "I've got my fingers crossed that Cam Jordan is going to take this time."

14

The view through the jet window behind Jon's head was of an inky black sky. Jon had let me sit in the aisle seat, knowing how I have this thing about confinement. In fact, I wondered how I'd manage to stay aboard the aircraft for the seven-hour flight to Venice without having a fit or trying to escape through a tiny porthole. I wasn't able to glimpse the midnight blue Atlantic below us but I knew it was there. When I started to wonder if crashing into the ocean would be preferable to crashing into land, I knew it was time to stop pondering the risks of flying and the improbability that this huge aircraft could remain aloft.

"Melanie had news," I told Jon. Melanie had driven me to the airport and had shared her latest with me.

Jon closed his magazine and turned to me. The reading light above his head illuminated his golden blonde hair causing it to shine like the heads of the saints in the book on Renaissance paintings I was perusing. I was giving myself a crash course in Italian art.

No matter how many times Jon looks at me, each time his face lights up. He doesn't do this with anyone but me. I know; I've checked. I love the way he glows as his eyes study my face. And sometimes he looks into my eyes so deeply, I feel our souls connect. I am able to feel pure joy pass from him to me. I love this feeling. For two years I'd been calling it friendship. Now I was calling it what it really was — love.

"What did Melanie have to say?" he asked, in no way aware of the intense longing for me that showed on his face.

"Well, you know her lawyer hired a private investigator. It seems that at about noon on the day of Joey Fielding's murder, a small boat was docked at the Bitterman's boat dock. The construction crew next door reported seeing it there. It didn't strike them as odd because boats tie up at the private docks along Harbor Island all the time."

"So someone could have come by boat to meet Fielding there. But how did Fielding get into the house? Did the PI find that out?"

"According to the police report he had a key to the Bitterman front door in his pocket. Brie Bitterman admitted to them that she'd given him a key," I said, repeating what Melanie had told me. Except that Melanie had gone into a tirade about Joey Fielding being secretly engaged to Brie Bitterman.

"She's a child, for God's sake," Melanie had complained. "What in the world was Joey doing with a child when he could have had a woman?"

"Did he find out who the gun belonged to?" Jon asked.

"She. Not he. Why does everyone assume a private investigator has to be a man?"

Jon held up his palms in pseudo surrender. "I apologize for my political incorrectness," he said in mock contrition. "She. Did she find out who the gun belonged to?"

"Yes," I said with an amused smile. "Al Shariff, Brie's manager."

"Well, I hope the detective is checking him out, where

he was at the time of the murder, does he have a strong alibi," Jon said. "Was there anything unprofessional about his relationship with Brie."

"Melanie's PI is going over his life with a fine-tooth comb. If he has anything to hide this woman will find it."

"What about fingerprints on the gun? Were Shariff's prints on it as well as Melanie's?" Jon asked.

"You'd think so, wouldn't you, but only Melanie's prints were on the gun. Somebody wiped it clean before she touched it."

I leaned back and closed my eyes. "I can't believe we're on our way to Italy. I can't tell you how much I've dreamed of going there, ever since I read Frances Mayes book about restoring Bramasole. This is going to be a long flight, I wish I could sleep."

I had worked a full day on Tuesday and then at nightfall Melanie had driven me to the airport where I'd met Jon. We'd flown to New York for our connection to Venice. Now it was the early hours of Wednesday.

Jon took my hand and I opened my eyes and looked into his.

"Ashley, there's a vast ocean down there. A really huge expanse of water that separates two continents. We're flying to one of those continents. We're leaving the other behind us, complete with all the problems that have plagued us recently. Melanie being charged with murder. The skeleton under the bottles. The grim ATF agent who is straight out of 'Dragnet.' Our odious client. Nick with his wanderlust and his infidelity.

"Just you and me and Italy makes three," he quipped. "Let's just think about us. About what makes us happy for the next few days. Our client, as much as we personally dislike him, has given us a golden holiday. Let's focus on that and on us, on our passion for historic architecture, our love of beautiful villas, on the sights we're going to see. Let's focus on each other."

I returned his joyous smile. He was right, as usual. I put my head on his shoulder and felt myself truly relax. Then I thought it was time to tell him something I had not told anyone yet, not even Melanie, something that I had scarcely acknowledged to myself.

"I had a visitor this afternoon while I was packing," I murmured, my eyes remaining closed. "A process server. Nick has started divorce proceedings. I have no reason to fight a divorce. So in a year, I'll be a single woman again."

I lifted my head and looked into his eyes to see his reaction. Jubilant? Triumphant?

What I saw there was concern, concern for me. He squeezed my hand as he regarded me solemnly. "I know how hard this is for you, Ashley. I know how you hate failure. But this is for the best and I think that deep down you know it is. It's time to let go."

"Yes," I whispered and rested my head on his shoulder again where to my astonishment I cat napped through the flight.

15

The unseasonably warm weather we had back home had followed us to Italy. Groggy and stiff from sitting in a seat all night, we staggered through customs and out into the late morning sunshine to find a cab. After we checked into the Hotel Firenze, all I wanted was a bed. No sightseeing for me, not until my aching body had lain prone for several hours. We didn't even take time to marvel at the hotel's sixteenth century architecture, barely glancing up at the marble facade with its iron arches. Later.

Taking the elevator to the fourth floor, I went to my room and Jon went to his. I closed the draperies and slept until mid-afternoon when Jon knocked on my door to rouse me.

"Hey, sleepy head, Venice awaits. Come on. Get dressed. I'll wait for you on the fifth floor balcony. Wear something pretty." He was gone.

Wear something pretty. Hmmmm. I had brought my girly clothes, leaving my work clothes at home. Melanie sarcastically refers to my khaki pants and denim shirts and my steel-toed construction boots as my "construction wear chic."

I unpacked a flirty skirt, a sweater set, and flat sandals. And in case the evening cooled down, a cashmere shawl that had belonged to mama. A quick shower, a flick of a hair brush, a touch of makeup and I was on the elevator to the fifth floor in less than thirty minutes.

Jon was at a table with a carafe of coffee. He stood when I approached and again his expression mellowed, telling me how happy he was to see me. "Hi gorgeous," he said, his customary greeting for me, and he buzzed my cheek. "You look pretty."

"I need some of that," I said.

"Be prepared. It's really strong. The Italians like it that way."

He filled my cup. "To us," he said.

"To us," I repeated, and took a sip. "Wow! That's powerful." But I drank it all and asked for another.

"Look at this view!" I exclaimed.

Our hotel was located in the historic center of Venice. The city stretched out below us. There was a gorgeous view of the basin and the San Marco basilica.

"I want to see the square," I said. "I'm ready."

"We'll find a sidewalk cafe there," Jon said, echoing my enthusiasm. "I'm hungry."

The Piazza San Marco — the famous St. Mark's Square — was a short walk from our hotel. Loggias lined three sides of the square, offering unobstructed views of St. Mark's basilica. Over the arched entrance were the four famous gilded bronze horses so life-like they looked like they might gallop off the facade and into the square at any moment. We walked inside the dusky cathedral to gaze around and to examine a white marble tomb where the remains of St. Mark reposed.

Next we toured the Doge's Palace, admiring paintings by Tintoretto and Veronese.

And there was the Bridge of Sighs that led into a prison.

"Everything looks just like it does in the movies," I said as we held hands and strolled through the crowds, peering into the windows of luxury shops and elegant hotels.

"It does," Jon marvelled. "Pigeons and all."

The pigeons flocked at our feet, and settled on statues and balustrades, and women in stalls rattled little packets of maize, inviting us to buy, to feed the pigeons.

"They built this square in the eleventh century," Jon said. "And there used to be a canal that flowed through it. We think we've got old at home, living in a city that was incorporated in 1739, but the culture here, think about it. And the architecture. It's so classically Italian Renaissance."

"It's harmonious. Everything looks like it belongs, not one jarring element. Oh! A free table. Grab it. I'm starving."

We hurried to a vacant table at an outdoor cafe.

"What's more Italian than pizza," Jon said. "That's what I'm having." He grinned.

I grinned back. "Me too. Pizza is perfect for breakfast, lunch, or dinner and I have no idea which meal this is. My internal clock is really messed up but, oh, this is fun!"

Our waiter spoke English. Everyone spoke English. We ordered chianti and pizza.

Jon reached across the table and took my hand. "I wouldn't want to share this experience with anyone but you."

I smiled into his eyes. "I feel the same way," I said, and meant it.

Who else loved the exact same things that I loved but Jon? We were a fit, I suddenly realized. We'd always been a perfect fit. He was my best friend, the person I had the most in common with, the person who knew me best, the person I trusted most.

As darkness settled, we held hands and wandered through the historic center of the city. People were out, men gathered on corners in little clicks, young mothers with strollers, children, dogs, old people. The city was alive, vital, as if everyone had turned out for a party. We marvelled at the sights, the beauty, the architecture, drinking it all in, memorizing so we wouldn't forget.

Jon took a few pictures but mostly we just looked. The camera seemed to intrude on our intimacy so he abandoned it.

Outside my room at the Hotel Firenze, he asked, "May I come in?" And he sounded shy.

"Of course," I replied. "I've got a small balcony. Let's go out there."

We stood on the balcony admiring the city lights, the lights from St. Mark's Square. We wrapped our arms around each and held each other as we admired the view, told each other, Pinch me so I'll know I'm not dreaming; we're really here. This is not a dream.

"It's always been you, Ashley," he murmured.

He pulled me closer. I snuggled in his arms, let out a long sigh, realizing I'd been holding my breath. I inhaled the smell of his neck. He smelled of aftershave and pizza and of sunshine.

And then I did something a part of me has been wanting to do for two years. I reached my arms up around his neck and lifted my face to be kissed.

And Jon kissed me. Our first kiss. His lips were soft but firm. Not demanding, not taking, just very giving. The kiss lasted for what seemed like an eternity because time stood still. I didn't want it to end, and I was glad he was holding me up because my knees started to buckle.

"Where did you learn to kiss like that?" I asked, surprised and thrilled at the same time.

He smiled at me. "It's easy when you're kissing the right person."

"Yes," I agreed and smiled so broadly I thought my jaw might break.

In the morning we hired a driver to take us to the five Palladio villas. Jon had not spent the night with me. Neither of us was ready for that. We were taking it slowly. There was plenty of time. Everything had to be right, and timing, I was discovering, was crucial to success.

We drove into the suburbs to see Palladio's Villa Rotonda. "Reminds me of Monticello," I said as we toured the grounds.

"I've seen pictures of this place," Jon said. "I can't believe I'm really seeing it in person. Andrea Palladio was probably the most influential architect of all time. He influenced Jefferson and classical American architecture. Why, even the houses being built today have Palladian windows."

Next we drove to the village of Maser to see the Villa Barbaro that had been built in 1558 on the ruins of a medieval castle. "And Palladio was influenced by the classic temples of Greece and Rome. Nothing new under the sun." Inside we admired more frescoes painted by Veronese.

We had lunch in the hilltown of Asolo in a small family-run restaurant. Again dining was *al fresco*. "Just like home," I told Jon. "What is there about eating out of doors that sharpens the appetite?"

"I'm glad you've got your appetite back. I was worried about you there for a while."

After lunch the Italians took siesta but Jon and I and our driver completed the Palladio tour. We were pressed for time. Tomorrow we'd drive to Lucca. As soon as we had known we were coming to Italy, we had agreed that a tour of Palladio's villas was something we had to do and so we had detoured to Venice.

We toured the Villa Emo, and La Mal Contenta with its Greek temple front. The source of the villa's name came from the name of the village, Malcontenta di Mira.

But by far, my favorite was the Villa Cornaro located in the village of Piombino Dese and owned by an American couple from Atlanta. The interior of the villa was magnificent with a statuary gallery that included full-figure statues of such personages as a Carnaro doge and his wife, the Queen of Cyprus. We wandered from lofty room to lofty room, where enormous pastel frescoes featured scenes from the Old and New Testaments.

Back at our hotel we separated, going to our rooms for a brief lie down, a shower and a change of clothes, then met again for dinner. We strolled over one of the many bridges that crisscrossed the canal and as luck would have it stumbled upon the Trattoria al Ponte. The bridges were arched with intricate iron railings, the kind of bridges where trolls hid in children's fairy tales. But there were no trolls here, only handsome gondoliers with thick black hair and flirtatious black eyes.

Our waitress was friendly and spoke enough English to describe the menu. She recommended Rabosco, a slightly fizzy local red wine that we lapped up with delight. I ordered spaghetti con scampi e radicchio and Jon had spaghetti Bolognese. For dolci we had galati, light and cool.

After dinner we cruised the canal in a gondola, snuggled together, kissed when the gondolier was not looking. "Italy is so romantic," I said.

"With you, it is," Jon replied.

My room was dark when we entered but we did not turn on the lights. Instead, I flung open the doors to the balcony so that ambient city light flowed into the room. From somewhere below a man was singing Italian ballads. We did not understand the words but the meaning seemed clear, a ballad about finding true love. The tenor's voice was rich and strong and he sang of burning desire as we held each other and made love, murmuring our own words of love.

16

During the night I dreamed I was wandering alone in a large manor house. The house was frightening and I was lost. The rooms were enormous with lofty ceilings and I moved from room to room searching for a way out. I knew Jon was there somewhere, but always in the shadows where I could not see him. When I came close to where he was concealed, he'd vanish into the next room.

I called for him to wait. "Jon!" I cried. "Wait for me. Don't leave me!"

I must have cried out in my sleep for Jon woke me. "It's all right, Ashley. I'm here. You're just having a bad dream." His arms went around me, holding me tight. "Sssshh," he whispered. "I have you now."

In the morning we rented a car and driver for the trip south to the Lucchese hills of Tuscany. The road wound through vineyards and olive groves, and valleys stretched for miles in every direction. The hamlet of Borgo Lucchese, our destination, was located just outside the ancient walled city of Lucca. "Lucca's famous walls were constructed in the sixteenth century," Jon paraphrased his guidebook, "but the city itself dates to the Paleolithic period. Etruscans lived there and then the Romans. The city reached its splendor during the period from the Middle Ages to the Renaissance."

"Imagine living with all this history," I commented, as our car followed a country lane deep into the countryside. "But the Italians must take it for granted just as we take our past for granted."

We entered Borgo Lucchese through a private entrance gate. Some of the buildings were made of stone but others had been rendered an incredible, soft salmon pink. "They're the color of my house back home," Jon remarked excitedly.

We checked in and were shown to our rooms by a servant. We were staying in a wild-boar hunting lodge called Ferro-a-u, the oldest building on the property with walls that were a thousand years old. Outside the lodge, lemon trees grew and their fragrance was lovely, citrusy and clean.

We unpacked and went to work. The sooner the work was done, the sooner we could play. The manager had been informed that we were old house restorers and that we were on assignment for David Boleyn.

"Mr. Boleyn," the manager said, "he is one of my best patrons. He brings guests here, many guests, famous people from your country, senators and congressmen, their wives. And husbands also. We give them a very nice holiday, very nice. Please go anywhere you wish, into any of the rooms and suites that are not occupied. And be sure you see the many common rooms."

While Jon took pictures with a 35mm camera, I made notes and drew sketches. Jon's camera was essential to our work, a camera that had been adapted for use with a photogrammetry computer program that analyzed pictures and calculated measurements.

The rooms were all beautifully decorated with original

beamed ceilings and terracotta floors. Many of the rooms had lovely soft hand-painted frescoes. The common rooms included a grand dining room and a formal drawing room, a music room, a card and billiard room, and a wine library.

Outside there were piazzas, seventeenth century fountains, and park lands.

Our unseasonably mild weather stayed with us and we had lunch in a courtyard next to the kitchen. The housekeeper served us wild mushroom lasagna, a hearty table wine, warm crusty bread. Pears steeped in sweetened red wine for dolci, dessert.

We entered the garden through a lovely arched walkway set in the center of a stone building which was originally the chapel. A shady gazebo stood before us, and beyond it lay a large expanse of green lawn that led to a pool. We strolled around the perimeter of the lawn, amid cypress trees, magnolias, and weeping willows.

"These trees are just like home," I said. "The grounds here remind me of Airlie Gardens."

We came to a lake with lilies and stately white swans floating on its surface.

"Just like the lagoons at Airlie," Jon said. "I think I might be getting homesick."

"Me too."

Jon turned me to face him, tracing the curve of my cheek with a fingertip. "Ashley, I have something to say. I've been rehearsing this speech ever since we left New York."

"Yes, Jon," I said lovingly, looking into his eyes.

"I've been in love with you for two years," he said, "ever since you returned home from college. I'm sick of eating my heart out over you. I want you to marry me, just as soon as you are free, and for us to make a life together. We'll have a good life. I've thought this through. We'll work together, we can live at your house downtown during the week and spend our weekends at Wrightsville at my beach house. Everything will be perfect. It will work out beautifully. But you've got to say yes."

I placed my hands on his chest as if to anchor him. "And I want to marry you, Jon. My answer is yes."

"Wow! Wonderful!" he exclaimed. "She said 'yes,'" he shouted, picking me up by the waist and spinning me around in a circular dance. The swans eyed us warily and swiftly glided to the far side of the lake.

"Then it's settled," he said, setting me on my feet. He seemed relieved, joyous. Had he been worried that I might say no? "Shall we tell them when we get home? Do you think Melanie will approve? How soon can I give you a ring?"

I laughed. "We can tell anyone we want. And yes, Melanie will approve. Melanie has been pleading your case all along. Melanie says we are a perfect match. And she pointed out that Daddy knew you when he was alive, that he thought you were wonderful, full of integrity, a man among men."

Jon beamed. I couldn't have said anything to make him happier. I thought back over the past two years. All the while I'd been caught up in the sizzling chemistry that passed for love between Nick and me, Jon had been right there, devoted and waiting for his chance.

I'd thought of him as a work partner, a buddy, a brother. Now I knew he was everything I wanted, and more.

"Let's wait a while on the ring," I said.

"How about Christmas?" he asked.

"Yes. I can't think of anything I want more for Christmas than your ring."

He took me in his arms, held me close, and kissed me. "The Italians have a charming custom for this time of day. It's called a siesta. They go to their rooms and sleep. But I have a feeling they do more than sleep. Let's find out."

"Jon, I want a baby," I blurted.

"I do too. Several, in fact," he responded as he took my hand and led me to our lodge.

"But I don't know if I can have them," I confessed.

"I want you, Ashley. I'll take my chances."

As it turned out he was right. There was more to do during siesta than sleep.

17

As our jet winged across the Atlantic, bringing us closer to home, discussion of the troubles that awaited us there could not be avoided.

At first we spoke of Italy, reminisced about the glorious light there, the gorgeous architecture, the ancient churches and the walled towns. We relived our romantic celebratory dinner of our last night in Lucca, our visits to the churches by candlelight. But as our plane kept pace with the sun's journey westward, we couldn't help speculating about what we'd find when we got home.

"Whoever killed Joey Fielding set Melanie up," I said.

"Well, everyone knew she was the real estate agent for the Bitterman house. Her sign was right out front. And Melanie's got a reputation as a hands-on realtor. So the killer didn't even have to know Melanie personally, just that she had a key to the house and that she'd be in and out frequently," Jon said.

"But they couldn't know that she wouldn't have a client with her. If she had taken a client, she could not be framed for murdering Joey," I reasoned. "So it must have been someone who was keeping track of her schedule, who knew she checked the house after lunch every day. Someone was watching the house. And maybe watching Melanie.

"Then he or she lured Joey Fielding there and shot him, placed the gun on the floor right inside the front door where Melanie would be sure to see it, and acting in her role as care-taker, she'd be sure to pick it up and put it in a safe place. He called the police as soon as he saw her enter the house, know-ing the police station was a minute away."

I agreed this is what had happened.

"But who did it and why?" I wondered out loud.

"We're going to get to the bottom of this," Jon said reas-suringly.

"I don't like it that Mickey Ballantine is still hanging around Wilmington, and that Melanie is harboring him, let-ting him hide out at her house."

"You know Melanie. She's loyal to her old friends. But I want you to be careful if you should encounter him again. I don't trust that guy. Never did, even if he did help us out that time."

"He won't be staying at Melanie's house again, not unless she lets him in. I made him give me her house key."

"Good move."

"But he's involved in some scam, Jon. He as much as told me so. Somebody owes him money, he said, and he's not leav-ing town until he collects it. Probably one of his gambling buddies but I have no idea who his friends are."

"Melanie might know," Jon suggested.

"Let's talk about who had access to the Bitterman house. Bunny and Clay, but they were in Palm Beach."

"Do we know that for a fact?" Jon asked. "Did the police check their alibis?"

"I'm not trusting the police to do any detecting on this case. They've charged Melanie with the crime, case closed as far as they are concerned and move on to the next."

I withdrew a notebook from my carryall. "Let's make a list of suggestions for Melanie's private investigator. Number one: verify that Bunny and Clay Bitterman were at Palm Beach on Thursday, November 3rd, the day of the murder." I wrote that down.

"Good thinking. Okay, next is Brie. Where was she? Melanie said she was back in the states, but where exactly?"

I made a note. "Then there's Al Shariff. His gun was the murder weapon. How did his gun get into the house if he did not take it there? Did he have a key to the house? Where was he that day? Does he have a strong alibi?"

I added Al Shariff to my list along with the questions.

"And here's another question that hasn't been answered: how did Joey Fielding get to the Bitterman house that day? His car is identical to Melanie's and no one saw it. Melanie said it was not there when she arrived."

My list was growing.

"He may have been the person who came by boat," Jon said.

"Or maybe they both did. He and his killer."

Jon said, "I can't help wondering about Scott Randolph and the case he's working on. ATF handles smuggling. Alcohol, tobacco, yes, but also firearms and explosives. And in today's world that means terrorists and the people who aid terrorists. At the risk of making another politically incorrect statement, Ashley, Shariff is of Middle Eastern descent, he's a Muslim, and he travels all over the world with Brie's tours. A perfect cover. How difficult would it be for him to smuggle firearms or explosives in the crates they ship for Brie's shows? There would be props, costumes, musical instruments. And Homeland Security does not check cargo the way they check passengers."

I looked at him with renewed admiration. "You're not

just a pretty face, are you?" I quipped, and we smiled and kissed.

"That's really good thinking, Jon." My list was growing longer. Investigate Al Shariff and his connections was the next item I wrote down.

"But if the ATF was in Wilmington investigating Shariff, wouldn't they have sent a whole team of agents?" I wondered.

"We don't know that they haven't, Ashley. We only know what Scott Randolph told us about the corpse we found on the Boleyn estate. We know nothing about his official reason for being in Wilmington or about the case he's investigating."

"No, we don't," I said thoughtfully. "Let's have the investigator check on him too. Verify his credentials."

I felt a bump as the landing gear was lowered. And the captain came on the intercom to announce that we were approaching New York.

Then it hit me. "You know, Jon, there's a flaw in our reasoning."

"There is?"

"We've been listing all the people who had access to the Bitterman house, but Joey Fielding had a key so he could have let anyone in. He could have arranged to meet someone there, knowing that the house was empty. Maybe someone he did not want to be seen with. So that broadens our scope, doesn't it?"

"Sure does. Broadens it to just about everyone in Wilmington!"

18

"I'm glad you're back, shug, I missed you," Melanie told me from the phone in her office where I'd located her at eleven on Sunday morning. "Did you have a good time?"

"Wonderful," I breathed. "Jon and I would like to see you this evening. We have something to tell you," I sang.

"And I know what it is," she sang back.

"We thought we'd like Cam to be there, too. We like him a lot, Mel, and think of him as a friend." Actually, Jon had him lined up to be our best man. And Melanie, of course, would be my maid of honor. When the time came. A year from now. A Christmas wedding, we had decided on the drive from the airport to my house last night. Jon had not stayed. We were both exhausted and needed a good night's rest.

Also we had decided we'd better behave discreetly on home turf because we had our reputations to think of — personal as well as professional.

Sunday was Melanie's busiest day but I hoped she'd make time for us. Our good news was too important to delay.

"Sure, I'll call Cam. I'm sure he'd love to come. I'm supposed to show a house at five and sometimes those showings run late, especially if the buyer is interested. And this is the second time she's seeing it so she is interested. I'll move the appointment up to this afternoon, and we'll all meet at my house at six for cocktails and dinner. How's that?"

"You're the best, big sis. Melanie? How have things been going here? Are the police still harassing you?"

"Actually, things have been going surprisingly well. My lawyer, Walt Brice, is running interference with the police and the D.A. And my regular clients are being amazingly supportive. Remember dear Mae Mae Mackie and Lucy Lou Upchurch? Well, those old dears are selling their lovely French provincial home out on the waterway and they just gave me the listing. Then they want me to find them something in an over 55 community. I just love those two darlings.

"And other society folk are coming 'round too. Solidarity, that's what I'm getting. I just love Wilmington." Then her tone changed to anger and she lashed out, "But I'm still going to sue someone when this is all over and those idiot police clear me!"

"What can I bring for dinner?" I asked, wanting to get her mood back on the upswing.

"Not a thing. I'll call the Bridge Tender and have them prepare something and I'll pick it up on my way home. How about that wonderful crab dip they make with garlic toast for an appetizer? And their tuna steak with horseradish is to die for. And I've got a good supply of white wine in the wine cooler."

"A feast," I said. "This will be fun."

"And Ashley, if I'm late, just let yourself in and set the table for me and uncork the wine, will you, shug? I'll be there by six."

"Of course. Love you, big sis."

"Back at you, little sis."

At five thirty it was already dark. I drove out Oleander to Greenville Loop Road, then on to Melanie's house on Sandpiper Cove.

My headlights picked out the opening in the fence and I maneuvered my Avalon down her sloping, sandy driveway. Melanie's garage door was shut so I didn't know if she had beat me home or not. Light shone diffusely from the windows in the master bedroom where I knew she left a lamp on for Spunky. I took my purse and stepped carefully down illuminated shallow steps to Melanie's small front porch. Pressing the doorbell, I heard soft chimes play inside. I waited but she didn't come. Maybe she's in the shower, I thought. I'd give her a minute; I didn't want to go barging in on her. Jon and Cam were due at six.

While I waited I gazed out over the porch railing into the dark backyard where the land dropped away to the cove and the boat dock where I'd seen Mickey Ballantine sail off soundlessly in a small boat. Lights from the Coast Guard Station at Wrightsville Beach flickered across Greenville Sound. Here in the woods, away from streets and traffic, the wind sighed and stirred piles of fallen leaves.

I took her house key out of my purse and let myself in. "Melanie," I called. No answer. So she wasn't here yet.

The small foyer was unlit. On my left lay the living room and it was dark too. A small glow of light shone down the hallway on the right which led to the bedroom wing.

I took a step inside. "Spunky? Here kitty, kitty."

I stepped in a wet, warm puddle. I had on open-toe high heeled sandals and my stockings soaked up the wetness. "Oh, Spunky," I said, disappointed. Spunky was usually a fastidious little soul who went only in his litter box. But when cats get resentful for being ignored or for being left alone for too long, they have been known to show you a thing or two with a deposit left right at the front door where you are sure to find it.

I reached for the light switch and turned it on. I was standing in a pool of blood!

"Melanie!" I screamed. I raced toward the bedrooms, my blood soaked sandals making bright red tracks on the white carpet. There were other blood tracks and streaks of blood. And the white wall was splattered with bright red spots. A blood bath had taken place here.

"Melanie!" I screamed again. I dug in my purse for my cell phone as I ran down the hall.

I rushed into the master bedroom. Melanie was lying face down, just inside the door. The back of her head was bleeding. Her beautiful auburn hair was matted and soaked with black blood. And the knife in her right hand dripped blood into the white carpet.

A short distance away, near the foot of the bed, Mickey Ballantine lay face up. His skin was dead white. He had lost a lot of blood. His chest and neck had been slashed repeatedly and viciously.

Dropping to my knees, I crawled over to Melanie's side. I felt her neck and let out a loud sigh of relief when I detected a pulse, feeble but steady. I punched in 911 on my cell phone, sobbing hysterically to the dispatcher that I needed an ambulance and the police.

While I waited for them, I stayed on my knees at Melanie's side, rocking back and forth, begging God to spare her life. As if in answer to my prayers, I suddenly realized I had to call Walter Brice. If the police allowed their suspicions to cloud their judgement as they had before, they'd jump to the wrong conclusion: that the knife in Melanie's hand meant she had killed Mickey Ballantine.

Walt was a neighbor, lived in the Greenville Loop neighborhood also. He answered my call on the first ring, and was at Melanie's house in three minutes.

19

The EMTs would not let me ride in the ambulance with Melanie. Jon and Cam arrived before the ambulance and the police and when Cam saw Melanie lying on the floor bleeding and injured, his skin turned a greenish color and his legs gave way. Jon steadied him, then picked me up and held me. He was white-lipped, shocked like Cam and me.

The EMTs and the police came all at once, all together, and took over. It seemed like all hell broke loose. They verified that Melanie was alive and that Mickey was dead. They started to question us but Walt made them stop.

"I'm going to the hospital with her!" I yelled at them.

Walt told them, "She'll be at the hospital. I'll give you their names and addresses. Call me when you want to question them and I'll set it up."

"You representing all these folks?" a detective whom I didn't know asked Walt, his tone dripping with sarcasm.

"For the moment, yes," Walt said firmly. "But they will have other counsel if needed."

Walt told the detective our names and addresses, then followed Jon, Cam and me out of the house. We left together for the medical center. Of the three of us, Jon seemed the most steady so he drove and we rode with him. Walt followed in his own car.

In the emergency unit we settled down to wait for word about Melanie's condition. While we waited, I gave Walt the list of suggestions for Melanie's private investigator that we had composed on the flight home from Italy.

After about an hour, the ER doc, a short, pugnacious black woman in green scrubs whom I would want on my side if I was injured, came to tell us that Melanie had a concussion but that she was awake.

I introduced myself as Melanie's sister, her only living relative. If need be I was prepared to act on her behalf, make decisions with her best interests in mind. But thankfully that was not necessary. Melanie was awake. Thank you, Jesus, I whispered under my breath.

"I had to shave the back of her head to stitch up the wound," the doctor told me. "I know Melanie Wilkes. She was our realtor. She sold my husband and me a house in Carolina Heights. We love it. But she's not going to be happy with me when she sees that bald spot on the back of her head."

I giggled nervously, knowing that if the doctor was concerned about Melanie's reaction to her head being shaved, then Melanie was not in grave danger. "But is she going to be okay?" I asked, needing to be reassured.

Jon and Cam leaned in close, hanging on her words.

"I think she'll be fine in a couple of days. She's young and healthy. But she's got to take it easy. We're transferring her to a bed and we'll keep her overnight."

She gave me a steely look, a "no one messes with me" look. "Now . . . about the police. They are hounding me about her head wound. I'll tell you what I told them in no uncertain terms: there is no way that head wound was self-inflicted. Somebody hit your sister, and hit her hard, with a heavy object. If I had to guess I'd say it was something like a heavy glass paperweight. There were no wood or rock fragments in the wound. The cause of the laceration was blunt force trauma. Her head was not cut by a sharp or jagged object but something round and smooth. A paperweight. Find it and you'll find the weapon."

"Melanie does have a paperweight that she keeps on the console in the foyer," I said excitedly. "She keeps it on top of the mail so that when the door opens, the draft doesn't blow papers on the floor."

The doctor was edging away, on her way to her next patient. "Then that's probably it. I've left instructions that the police may not question her until tomorrow."

"Thank you, doctor," I called.

"One of you take her home with you tomorrow. She has to be looked after," the doctor said.

"I will," I said.

The doctor gave us a little wave, trotted off, but called over her shoulder, "They'll let you know when she's settled in a room and you can see her then. But one at a time. She's had enough excitement."

Walt said, "She wouldn't be able to get into her house anyway. The police will have it sealed; it's a crime scene."

"And we can't let her see all that blood," Cam said.

"I'm going to have that carpeting ripped out of there as soon as the police will let me," I said.

"I'd better be going," Walt said. "Give her my best. Tell her I'll be back tomorrow and that I'll be with her when the police question her."

Melanie's head was elevated. She looked pale and frightened. I've never seen Melanie feeble before. Never even seen her sick. She had the constitution of a pack horse: strong, resolute, always carrying more than her share of weight. Seeing her frail like this shook me to the core of my being.

It was after midnight and quiet in the halls. I had told the nurses I was spending the night with her. Cam had already been in to see her, spoken to her softly, told her he loved her. He and Jon were waiting in the lobby for me to report back to them.

"No one will tell me what happened," she whispered.

I pulled my chair closer to her bed. I would have climbed up on the bed with her but did not want to jostle her for fear of causing her more pain. She seemed to want to talk.

"I don't know what happened," she repeated. "Tell me what happened."

So as delicately as possible I told her that Mickey Ballantine had been killed in her house, and that whoever did it was trying to set her up again by putting the knife in her hand.

"But this time it isn't going to work," I declared. "You are as much a victim as Mickey. Any fool can see that."

"Poor Mickey," Melanie said softly. "What is going on, Ashley, what is this all about? First Joey, then Mickey."

"We've got a killer on the loose," I said. "Now maybe the police will go after the real perp."

I couldn't help thinking what a fine homicide detective Nick had been before his ambitions had outstripped his good sense. Nick would have stuck with Joey's case, would have followed every lead until he was absolutely certain he had the right person.

"I didn't see a thing," Melanie said. "I came in through the garage like I always do. I snapped on the lights in the kitchen. I set the bags of take-out on the counter. That's the last thing I remember."

So her attacker had dragged her into the bedroom after he had knocked her unconscious. Mickey's body was already there, he was already dead when Melanie surprised the killer. Or had he lain in wait for her in the dark house? Waited so he could put the knife in her hand and try to make it look like Melanie had killed not once but twice? Perhaps he had intended to strike Melanie on the temple, to knock her out and make it look like a self-inflicted wound. Maybe she had turned her head as he struck.

"The kitchen light was off when I got there. He turned it off. I'm taking you to my house tomorrow." I told Melanie. "We've got to stick together, take care of each other. There is a killer out there and he's set on pinning the blame on you."

"Oh, I just want to go home to my dear little house on the cove," Melanie cried.

"You can't, Melanie," I said fiercely. "You can't go back there. It's a . . . " Mess was what I wanted to say. I settled for, "crime scene. The police will probably be back again tomorrow. Look, Mel, when they are finished, I'm going to have the carpeting stripped out. I don't want you to see it."

"That bad?" she asked in disbelief. "Can't we have it shampooed?"

"Melanie, you don't want it. We decorated that house together seven years ago. Remember how much fun we had. Now it's time to redecorate."

She had no idea how bad it was. We'd have to repaint because there were blood splatters on the wall.

I tried to get her mind on to something pleasant. "You know you've got hard wood floors under that carpeting and hard wood floors are in vogue again. Let's strip them and bleach them. Repaint. Recover the furniture. Redo everything."

"Okay," she said drowsily. Then her eyes fluttered open. "You didn't get to tell me your news. Remember, we were going to celebrate something tonight."

How sweet she was to think of me at a time like this.

"Jon and I are going to get married when I'm free. Nick filed for a divorce, Melanie. He is really through with me."

"That scoundrel," she hissed. "Oh, I can't keep my eyes open another second." But they snapped open again. "Spunky! Is he with you?"

"Oh my gosh, Spunky! No," I said, realizing guiltily that in all the excitement I'd forgotten all about him. "I didn't see him. He must have been hiding."

"Well, You've got to go back there and find him, Ashley! My poor baby. He'll be scared out of his wits with police all over the house. Why, he might have even run outside."

Tears slid down her cheeks.

I jumped up. "I'm going right now," I said, and nearly ran from the room. If he was outside, he'd be terrified.

20

"There is no way you are going back to that house alone," Jon declared. "I'm driving you."

"I'm going too," Cam said. "It'll be better than sitting around here. Melanie's asleep. I'll be back in the morning, hopefully with good news that we've found Spunky. She's crazy about that cat."

"Surely the police will have left by now," I said. "I don't want to have an encounter with them."

At one in the morning the medical center parking lot was quiet as we made our way to Jon's black Escalade. Soon we were flying down Seventeenth Street to Shipyard Boulevard, then on to Holly Tree Road and Greenville Loop. We turned right off of Greenville Loop Road onto Old Military Road and were soon rolling into Melanie's driveway.

The house was lit up like an ocean liner, every light in the house blazing. Yellow crime scene tape had been strung along the fence and among the trees, across the garage door, and looped over the porch rail. But no cops!

"Hallelujah!" I told Jon. "The cops are gone."

I got Melanie's house key out of my purse, we lifted the tape and slipped under it, and I let us in the front door. "Careful where you step," I warned, recalling how I'd stepped into a pool of blood. We entered cautiously and looked around.

"Good lord, this is a disaster," Cam said. "Ashley, we cannot let Melanie see her house in this condition. We've got to keep her away."

"We will. And just as soon as the cops give me the okay, I'll have Willie Hudson strip out the carpeting and paint those blood-splattered walls. We'll crate up her furniture and put it in storage. Redo everything. Make it look different."

Already I was moving to the hall closet for Spunky's cat carrier. "Guys, start searching. Pretend you're a cat. Where would you hide?"

"I'll take the bedroom wing, Cam," Jon said, "you take the dining room and living room. Don't worry, Ashley, we'll find him."

The take out dinner from the Bridge Tender Restaurant filled two white shopping bags on the kitchen counter where I sat the car carrier. The food had been sitting out for over five hours and I suspected it had spoiled. I dumped the contents — styrofoam boxes and plastic containers — into a plastic garbage bag, sealed it, and stuffed it into the trash can.

I used the shopping bags to load up with Spunky's Fancy Feast cans, his water bowl, his favorite food bowl, his play mouse. When that was done, I walked down the hall to find Jon.

The trails and footprints of blood on the carpeting had dried to rust-like brown streaks. He had dragged Mickey back here, Melanie too, I thought, as I stepped into the master bedroom. He had staged the entire scene. The carpet here was wet where Mickey had lain and bled to death.

A fine black dust residue coated the furniture surfaces; crime scene technicians had dusted for fingerprints.

Cam stuck his head in the door and let out a groan. "This is dreadful, worse than I remember. I was only focussed on Melanie before. Well, Spunky's not anywhere in the front rooms. I'm going to take a walk around outside. He knows me. I think he'll come if I call."

"Okay," I said. "I'll search here." I lifted the bed skirt, got down on my hands and knees and looked under the bed. "Here, Spunky, come out, kitty," I called.

I opened Melanie's closet door and looked inside. No sign of the cat. I got down Melanie's luggage from the top shelf and started packing. Her clothes, her makeup and toiletries from the adjoining bathroom. No sign of Spunky there. I emptied her dresser drawers — slips, underwear, tee shirts — and filled three suitcases. I was taking everything. I did not want her coming back here. I hoped the police were through, that they were not coming back, and that they'd never know we had trespassed at a crime scene.

Jon came in, stepping carefully, skirting the patches of blood-soaked carpeting. "Let's not forget her computer," I told him.

I paused with a nightgown in my hands, about to fold it into the suitcase on the bed. Something was bothering me. "How did he get in?" I asked Jon.

"Which one?" Jon asked me.

"Well, both. How did Mickey get in? I made him give me Melanie's house key. Did he break in? Melanie wasn't here to let him in. She came later. Mickey and the killer were already here inside the house when she got home. Mickey may have been dead at that point."

I stopped to consider. "She said she came in through the garage. She always closes the garage door behind her with the remote. She came directly from the garage into the kitchen. Jon, go into the garage and take a look around. See if someone broke a window in the garage or the side door."

While he was gone, I looked under furniture and scoured the rooms Jon had already searched. When I went back into Melanie's bedroom, Spunky was curled up on Melanie's nightgown in the top of her suitcase.

The sound of our voices had brought him out from his hiding place. "Oh, Spunky, you really gave us a scare."

I lifted him and stroked him, reassuring him with my voice. He meowed at me, plaintively, pitifully. "You saw it all," I said to him. "What did you see?"

I carried him out to the kitchen and put him into his cat

carrier on the kitchen counter. He must have felt safe in it because he did now howl, but curled up comfortably and watched us.

The fruit bowl on the counter caught my eye just as Jon came in from the garage and Cam came in through the front door.

"No sign of him out there . . . oh, you found him. Thank goodness."

Jon said, "The window and the door were securely closed and locked. And I checked the sliding glass doors earlier. No signs of a forced entry. Yet somehow one of them got in and probably let the other in."

I reached into the fruit bowl.

"What are . . . ?"

"Just a minute," I said. The bowl was filled with fresh fruit, replacements for the fruit that had been there last weekend. But the key was still at the bottom of the bowl where I'd dropped it, hidden under the fruit.

I held it up. "This is the key I took from Mickey Ballantine. I asked him for Melanie's house key and he gave it to me."

I left the kitchen, crossed the foyer, opened the front door and inserted the key in the lock. "Son of a gun! It doesn't fit. He scammed me."

Jon and Cam had followed me into the foyer. "So," Jon said, "he still had Melanie's house key. And he used it to let himself in and to possibly let his killer in as well. He didn't know Melanie would be coming home early."

"And so he was meeting someone here," Cam finished.

"And that someone killed him," I said. "Then tried to pin the blame on Melanie. If only Spunky could speak. He knows."

I turned to go back into the kitchen for the cat carrier. "Will you guys get her luggage and her computer," I asked.

I had forgotten to check for the paperweight. "It's gone," I said, "the paperweight is gone. The ER doc must have told the police her theory and they took it to do their luminal testing."

Jon said, "Even if the killer washed it, blood traces will still show up under a lumalight. You can't wash blood away."

21

"None of them has an alibi that will hold up in court," Walter Brice, Melanie's defense attorney, declared.

We were gathered in my flower-filled library late on Monday afternoon. Cameron Jordan had bought out every florist in town and had the flowers delivered to Melanie's hospital room that morning. When she was discharged later that afternoon, we had settled her in the backseat of Jon's Escalade for the drive to my house. Cam drove a small sports car which was not very practical for transporting the convalescent Melanie and every floral arrangement in the city of Wilmington. The flowers had occupied every spare inch of my van; the interior would smell like flowers for days to come.

Now Melanie was tucked under a cozy afghan on my roomy leather sofa, the pain in her head vanquished by powerful meds that made her drowsy. Spunky slept at her feet, the effects of his recent trauma apparently nullified by the reappearance of the love of his life. We lesser mortals — Walt, Cam, Jon, and I — were having drinks as Walt reported his private investigator's findings.

"Our investigator flew to Palm Beach to verify the

Bittermans' alibi that they had spent that day together in their condo as they told the police. Apparently our police department doesn't have the budget to fly an officer to Florida to check an alibi. Well," he drawled, tenting his fingertips, "it seems a neighbor saw Mr. and Mrs. Bitterman drive off early the morning of November third. Mrs. Bitterman was behind the wheel. When she returned home less than an hour later she was alone. Where would we get our leads were it not for bored, nosy neighbors?"

Walt was in his mid-fifties, large and powerful looking with a take-charge personality, and balding. He had shaved his head clean, opting for the current power look among executives.

"According to the neighbor, Mr. Bitterman did not return until the next day. Mrs. Bitterman remained in the condo while he was gone."

"Wonder why they lied? What are they hiding?" I asked.

"What about Brie?" Melanie murmured. "Ashley, the light hurts my eyes. Will you snap that lamp off, please, shug."

"Are you sure you don't want me to put you to bed, sweetheart?" Cam asked.

"I'm going to try to stay awake a little bit longer," she said and smiled faintly. "I want to hear Walt's news."

She had dark circles under her eyes, her unwashed hair was stringy, and there was a bandage taped to the crown of her head like a yarmulke, still by the adoring looks Cam cast her way, in his eyes she was as ravishing as ever.

"Ah yes, Brie," Walt said. "Now this is very interesting. Brie claims she was in a meeting in Charlotte on the day Joey was killed, but she won't say who she was meeting with. She refused to tell the cops, and since their position is that she is not a suspect, they are letting the matter go. For now."

"What do you want to bet that Clay was with her that day. That he flew to Charlotte to attend this mysterious meeting," Jon speculated.

"But why? Why would he attend and why would he refuse to tell the police about it?" I asked.

Walt waited patiently for us to get it.

"Wait a minute," I almost shouted, "Brie is underage. She would not be able to sign contracts. She'd need her father to sign for her. That's it, isn't it?" I asked Walt.

He grinned. "That's what we think."

"But why make a mystery of it? And what about Ali Shariff? Did he attend this meeting?" Jon asked.

Cam sipped his drink and kept an eye on Melanie who was nodding off. "I'm taking her to her room," he said. He was tall and rangy and apparently stronger than he looked for he lifted Melanie easily from the sofa and carried her toward the stairs.

She awakened. "What?" she murmured.

I heard Cam say suggestively, "I'm taking you to bed, sweetheart." Followed by my sister's soft coy giggle.

Spunky awoke, sprang from the sofa, and trailed after them out of the room.

Walt smiled benignly and Jon and I exchanged looks. Us next, I thought, and caught his look of agreement.

"According to this report, the investigator believes Shariff was unaware of the meeting," Walt answered.

"Oooooh," I said. "The meeting was about him. Were they going to replace him, I wonder."

Walt replied, "We don't know. Shariff told the police he was at home in his apartment in Wilmington. And guess where he lives? Same apartment complex in Monkey Junction as Joey Fielding. Could be a mere coincidence. It's a very large complex. He made many phone calls but they were from a cell phone and could have been made from anywhere. He doesn't have an alibi. Done of them do."

"You know what this means, don't you?" I said. "Shariff

moves higher on my suspect list. What if he was envious of Brie's coming marriage to Joey? Maybe he feared Joey would exert an enormous influence on Brie, maybe even take over the management of her career, leaving Shariff out in the cold."

"That's a distinct possibility," Jon said. "What do we know about Shariff, Walt? How does he explain his gun being in the Bitterman house and used as the murder weapon?"

"He doesn't explain how it got there," Walt said. "His story is the gun had been stolen several months ago."

"Did he file a report with the police?" I asked.

Walt shook his head negatively. "Said he didn't bother. Too busy."

Walt consulted the report again. "Shariff was small potatoes until he met Brie Bitterman. Discovered her singing at Mickey Ballantine's club downtown at age fifteen and recognized her talent. Got her voice lessons, and acted as her coach and agent. Got her bookings in major Southern cities, recording sessions, and she took off. He's made a bundle on her talent."

"A bundle that he wouldn't want to share with Joey Fielding. Or any other man," Jon said.

"Was there anything romantic between Shariff and Brie?" I asked. "He's much too old for her too, at least by twenty years. But then Joey Fielding was too old for her, in my opinion. He was close to ten years older than she. There's a big difference between seventeen and twenty-six."

"Brie appears to be mature for her age," Walt said. "She worked the clubs at age fifteen while keeping her grades up in school. Ambitious even then. Driven. Doesn't drink. No drugs."

"I still don't get it," Jon said. "If the secret meeting was strictly to hire another agent, why would she refuse to tell that to the police? It must have been bigger. Maybe new production people, a new tour, and she's keeping it under wraps until the contract is signed, sealed, and delivered."

"My thoughts exactly, Jon," Walt said, nodding his agreement.

I reached down into my purse on the floor near my chair. "This is the key Mickey Ballantine gave me when I asked him to return Melanie's house key."

I handed the key to Walt. "This is not Melanie's key. It did not fit any door in her house. I think you ought to have it. I don't know what it unlocks but it might be important to the investigation."

Walt slipped the key into an envelope and labeled the envelope. "I'll see what I can learn. So far, the police are not aware that you returned to Melanie's house and took her clothes. If they do discover that, we may have a problem on our hands. They could charge you with obstruction in a homicide investigation."

"But why would they go back to the house?" I asked. "Haven't they concluded their forensic investigation? Jon, Cam, and I walked all over the carpeting before the police arrived. So did the EMTs and the first officers on the scene. Surely, there's nothing they can learn from an examination of the carpeting.

"Walt, I want to have that carpeting stripped out of there. I never want Melanie to have to see evidence of the carnage that took place in her home. She loves that house. Would you see if you can get us permission to get back into the house just as quickly as possible?"

"I understand and I'll do my best," he replied.

"And, Walt, here's something that has been bothering me. How did Joey Fielding get to the Bitterman house the day he was killed? His car is identical to Melanie's and no one saw it. Melanie said it was not there when she arrived. But the construction crew next door said there was a small boat docked at the Bitterman's pier. So did Joey Fielding come by boat? And if so, did he come alone?"

"I don't have the answers to those questions yet, Ashley. And I won't know what the cops know until we get to the discovery phase of this case, which may be some time from now. The D.A.'s office is going after this one with a sledge hammer. They want to nail Melanie. But so far all they've got is sloppy investigative work."

"Fielding's killer may have come on the boat with him," Jon said, "so it's important that your P.I. talk to everyone in the Point Place area."

Walt made a note on his legal pad, then said, "We can't find a thing about Scott Randolph. Don't know if he is a legitimate agent or what. I've got contacts in the local FBI offices and they usually have a pretty good idea about what is going on. They never heard of him, and don't know anything about an ATF investigation going on here."

"Could he be undercover?" Jon asked.

Walt shook his head. "I don't know. As of now we don't have a clue. But I'll keep on it."

Jon said, "I have to ask this. Does Shariff have ties to any of the extremist Muslim groups? Could he be the target of a secret ATF investigation?"

Walt replied thoughtfully, "We'll keep working on this one. We're still nosing around. It's still early in the game."

"I hope Dr. McAllister is having better luck with her mystery than we are with ours," I said.

22

"Believe me, Ashley, I have my priorities straight," Cameron Jordan told me the next morning. "We could all be blown away by terrorists tomorrow or die of the bird flu next year."

"How true," I responded.

He continued explaining his arrival at my front door at seven a.m. "I'm in love with that lady upstairs, have been since the first time I laid eyes on her. So I'm here because I *want* to take care of her. So scoot! Go on to work. I know they need you out at the Boleyn estate."

"You're a great guy, Cam. But who's going to run Gem Star Studios if you're here playing nursemaid to Melanie?" I asked.

"Oh, I can handle that from here," he said breezily. "That is if you don't mind my setting up in your library. I'll get some teckies out here from the studio with a communication system. Then I can do live teleconferencing with my staff when a decision has to be made. Okay with you?"

"Sure, make yourself at home, Cam," I said, marvelling at how technology was simplifying our lives. "Now, I've stocked the fridge with food that will be easy for her to eat. Her meds are in her room. But by this time, she's going to be chomping at the bit, starting to feel pretty restless that she can't get up and go. You know Melanie, she's got only one speed, and that's fast. Still, she's got to give her head time to heal."

Cam laughed. "I know, I know, Ashley. Go on. Get out of here. I'll confiscate her cell phone if that's what it takes to prevent her from wheeling and dealing from her sick bed. And if she gets a glimpse of my communication system she'll figure out a way to show houses from your library." Cam hooted. "She's a pistol. But that's my girl."

I went out the door wondering if Melanie was indeed his girl. I sure hoped so. He was the best thing for her — the best man to come into her life in years — yet she had still managed to get involved with guys like Mickey Ballantine and Joey Fielding. What was with her? And was I any better? Had we inherited self-destruct genes or what?

Mama had always been fey but sweet, other worldly and retiring. But even Mama had had the good sense to select a fine man and stick with him. My mother and father had been madly in love. It was obvious to anyone who saw them together. Still Mama did go off the deep end on a regular basis when she got bitten by the green-eyed monster.

I drove to the Boleyn estate feeling guilt free. Melanie was in good hands. It was now mid-November and the weather was cooling down to what passes for fall here on the coast, red leaves dropping into raggedy heaps under dogwood trees. As I pulled into the driveway off of Airlie Road, I caught sight of the hunting lodge. Crenelated tower, low pitched roof, wide eaves — all crumbling. I'd been driving past this site all of my life. There was something romantic and fairytale-like about the lodge's tower poking above the tree line, like the battlement of some medieval castle. You'd expect it to have a moat.

Two large branches had fallen from a live oak tree and lay at the side of the narrow lane. I wondered if there had been a storm while I was in Italy and assumed that Willie had dragged them off of the roadway.

Jon's Escalade parked in the high grass indicated he was somewhere on the property although I did not see him. But renovation work was underway, with ladders extended to the roof and scaffolding spanning the exterior walls. There was an electronic lift stacked with roofing tiles.

Willie Hudson came out to greet me as I stepped down from the van. "Hey, Miz Wilkes, good to have you home."

"Hi, Willie," I said. "It's good to be home. How are things going here?"

"Good. Good. Now what's this I hear about you finding that man stabbed to death and your sister being attacked by the killer? All over the papers, it was. Lordy, lordy, Miz Wilkes, you do have a talent for turning up them dead bodies."

His words stung and I winced but I knew that Willie did not intend to offend. In fact, he was one of the kindest souls I knew. Meticulous in his work and proud of the results, with deep roots in the black community and a steadfast commitment to his family and friends, to his church. Another man who had his priorities in order.

"And how is the other Miz Wilkes?" he asked kindly.

"Melanie's going to be all right," I answered. "She has a concussion but she's mending. The hard part will be keeping her down."

"Know about that, I do," Willie said, nodding his head vigorously. "And what about you, Miz Wilkes? You okay? Must have been a real shock for you, finding them that way. Paper say there was blood all over."

"It was dreadful, Willie." Then I asked about his wife, his sons and grandsons, many of whom were now up on the roof, patching holes, working with the Italians to replace broken and missing terracotta tiles.

"Looks like they made good progress while I was away," I said.

"Goin' good, Miz Wilkes. We've been lucky with this nice dry weather. If it holds long enough for us to get that roof repaired, we'll be in good shape. When the winter rains set in, we can be working inside. Come here, I want to show you something."

Willie led me to an exterior wall under the scaffolding where his crew had succeeded in removing almost all of the crumbling stucco. "Good solid brick walls under that stucco. See, they're a foot deep. They've held up well over the years. Sure, there's some damage but nothing we can't repair. We'll start applying the stucco this afternoon. Make hay while the sun does shine, I always say. Get that done and the roof repaired and the inside will be snug as a bug over the winter months."

Of course Jon and I had discovered that the outside walls were a foot in depth when we'd make our initial survey of the lodge. But I refrained from telling Willie that; let him think it was his discovery and that he was offering me good news.

"The windows have been on order for a month, Willie," I said. "They should be delivered any day now." The original window frames had rotted and fallen out, leaving tall, narrow apertures in the exterior walls through which rain and wind had entered the structure causing considerable damage inside. Jon had designed the window frames and they were being custom built, a rush order, but we gave the firm a lot of solid business so they were accommodating.

"The same company has a cast-iron and press-metal workshop. They are making the brackets and cornices from the impressions we took from the few remaining decorative elements." Most of the exterior trim was missing. "But there's no rush on that," I continued. "We can install them later after the structural repairs have been made." Willie knew all this but we liked to discuss things, bring each other up to date.

With our semi-tropical climate we were able to work outside almost year round. About January we'd go into a cold, rainy season and it would be good if all of our exterior work was completed by then.

"There's a lot missing from the inside," Willie said, as we walked into the shadowy interior.

"Yes," I agreed. "There have been vandals, and people have been helping themselves to anything they could pry loose and haul out of here for years."

Willie indicated a door. "No doorknobs. No key plates. All gone. Every door in this house. Looters," he said and looked disgusted.

I brightened. "As it happens, Willie, I have a collection of antique doorknobs and key plates that I've been buying from Architectural Salvage over the years."

Architectural Salvage was run by the Historic Wilmington Foundation to raise money and to recycle architectural artifacts, saving them from ending up as landfill.

"I think they'll fit and do nicely here." I lifted my head and looked upward to the second story where great gaps in the ceiling let the second floor show through and where streams of sunlight glanced down through holes in the roof.

"Jon says we've got close to 8000 square feet here," I said. "And I like the way the rooms open to the east and to the water. Beautiful views. We'll build a long brick terrace on this side and cover it with pergolas, the way they do in Italy. This is really going to be some house when we get finished with it."

I loved my work. I loved taking a building that was practically falling down and raising it up again, restoring it to its former glory.

"And they didn't make off with that German nickel sink

145

in the kitchen. Probably didn't think it was of value. Now that is a treasure to hold on to."

There was a carved wooden plaque above the doorway that led to the library that miraculously had been spared rain damage, probably because it was tucked under a deep ceiling cornice. I narrowed my eyes to get a better look at it. "We'll have to clean that up," I said. "If I am not mistaken that is a carving of Diana the Huntress." At her side, leaning against her legs, was a greyhound. "So they didn't get all the good stuff after all."

"Too high up," Willie commented. "We'll bring scaffolds in here when we're restoring these interior walls.

Diana was the Italian goddess of hunting. She was also a deity of fertility, invoked by women in ancient times to aid with conception and childbirth. That made me think of my own situation and to wonder if I'd continue to have miscarriages the way Melanie said that Mama had between our births. But Mama had given birth to two healthy babies so I looked upon that as a hopeful sign for me.

There were intricate decorative carvings throughout the lodge; most were difficult to decipher under an accumulation of dirt. Bookcases in the library were decorated with moldings showing animal motifs, the game that would have been hunted here — ducks, foxes, waterfowl.

The paneling in the banquet hall was badly damaged and would require a great deal of work to save. I imagined that in the lodge's heyday the walls had been adorned with the heads of bucks and other animals that were taken down by idle "gentle" men." I hoped that Crystal Lynne Boleyn's decorating tastes did not run to the heads of fallen wildlife.

I wandered down a hallway of successive arches searching for Jon and when I couldn't find him, I returned to Willie at the front of the house. Remembering the branches that had fallen, I asked, "Say, Willie, did you have a storm here while we were away? I noticed that big oak near the road lost a few branches."

"No, ma'am, no storm. Some big sixteen wheeler drove in here and ripped those branches off that tree. Must've been at night because it wasn't during the day when we were here. Circled all around the property, all the way out to the water, made a big U turn."

"What?" I asked in disbelief.

Willie motioned toward the waterway. "Go look for yourself. You can still see the ruts in the grass if you go out there and look. That driver sure must have been lost to come all the way in here to turn around," Willie said, shaking his head.

"When are those Italians coming to restore the terrazzo floors?" Willie asked. He pronounced Italians as Eye-talians, and I detected a certain amount of contempt in his voice.

"Are things working out okay with the crew that is helping you with the roof?" I asked.

"Yeah, sure, they're okay." Still Willie prided himself that he and his crew were able to handle most aspects of a restoration project themselves.

"Let's have the tile guys after we've done just about everything else. No point in restoring floors if we are still doing carpentry work above them."

Willie caught himself as he remembered something he had to tell me. "Oh, by the way, two nice fellers came in here looking for you. They said to tell you they got the antique bottles from the doctor and thanks a lot. I know what that's about: that body you found in the shed."

He shook his head again and grinned. "Don't know I want to be hanging out with you too much, Miz Wilkes. You sure are a magnet for murder!"

I gave him a playful shove in the shoulder, got in my van and drove over to Airlie Gardens. The gardens were officially closed for the winter but I knew some of the maintenance crew and they would let me park near the maintenance buildings. I pulled my van into an out-of-the-way parking space and got out.

I was starting a walking regime, as of today. All that pasta I'd had in Italy was filling out my waistline. Instead of lunch from now on, I'd come here to walk. Walk away my extra pounds. By my wedding day I would be as svelte as Melanie. And with a lover in my life again, I wanted to give him something special to hold on to. I didn't know what Nick's new girlfriend looked like, but when it came to the figure department, I decided, no one was going to look better than me.

23

I opened the door to my house as lively voices drifted from the library. A silky Southern drawl, like warm marmalade drizzled on toast. Aunt Ruby's voice. Melanie's light laughter, followed by a male's deeper voice. Binky was here too.

I rushed into the library to say hello, to be exclaimed over and smothered with hugs and kisses.

"What are you two doing here?" I asked. "Not that I am not thrilled to see you," I hastened to assure them.

"We've come to take care of dear Melanie," Aunt Ruby replied as she and Binkie resumed their seats in wing chairs across from the leather sofa where Melanie lay. "And to help you girls in whatever way we can."

"Darling Cam was able to return to running Gem Star Studios," Melanie explained, "now that Binkie and Aunt Ruby are here."

Darling Cam? Oh, that endearment was music to my ears.

Our mother's family, the Chastains, had settled in Savannah in the nineteen hundreds. Our father's family, the Wilkeses, were old time Wilmingtonians. Aunt Ruby still lived in the Chastain family home. She and Binkie divided their time between Savannah and Binkie's snug bungalow on Front Street.

During World War Two my maternal grandfather — Mama and Ruby's father — had moved to Wilmington to work on the Liberty ships. As Aunt Ruby had once explained the move to Melanie and me: "During the war years Daddy — your grandaddy — was valuable to the war effort as a shipyard foreman. Of course, we had naval yards in Savannah too, but Daddy went where he was needed. And where Daddy went, Mama went, and we girls too."

Aunt Ruby was a retired registered nurse, in her early seventies, but a role model for us all. She was vibrant and active — laced up her Reeboks every day, rain or shine, and walked for two miles, wore make-up and colored her hair.

She and Binkie had been married over the Labor Day holiday weekend. And from the way he couldn't take his eyes off her, he was as smitten with her now as he had been then, indeed had been for all of his life. Theirs was an unusual love story which dated back to childhood days.

Binkie smiled at me encouragingly, his fair skin crinkling, his seventy-year-old blue eyes as bright and keen as a seventeen-year-old's. He still dressed with his own inimicable flair: a favorite brown and cream herringbone tweed jacket that I remembered well; brown corduroy slacks that looked soft and comfortable; brown suede Hush Puppies.

He reached out and cradled my hand in both of his. His hands were worn like everything else about him, but offered reassurance and comfort. After Daddy died, Binkie stepped into my life and I leaned on him. He seemed to need someone to need him, for he had never married and had no family. Until Aunt Ruby re-entered his life.

"I've missed you, Ashley dear," he said now.

Binkie is Benjamin Higgins, Professor Emeritus at UNC-W's History Department. No one knows more about the history and folklore of the Lower Cape Fear region. He has authored many a scholarly book on the subject. With his friends — with everyone — he was kindly and gracious, a Southern gentleman of the old school, living a solitary life with his books and his legends.

And then last spring Aunt Ruby had been visiting us here in Wilmington and she and Binkie had rediscovered each other. They'd learned that neither had married anyone else. The sixty years that they had been separated drained away as smoothly as sand in an hourglass.

And now as if remembering their childhood, they began to speak of Lumina, the famous dance pavilion on Wrightsville Beach where they had met.

"I shall never forget that magical place," Aunt Ruby said. "Will you, Benjamin?"

"Never," he replied. "That's where I met you."

"Oh, the music," Aunt Ruby reminisced. "Jimmy Dorsey, Kay Kyser, the great band leaders all came to *Lumina*. And local talent was featured too.

"And once a week, there would be a children's dance," she said in a hushed, honeyed drawl, recalling her youth, and her favorite dancing partner. "On other nights, we children would be allowed to play outside on the beach and watch the grown-ups dance."

"And don't forget," Binkie reminded, his eyes twinkling merrily, "watch for German submarines."

"Oh, I do remember that. How much I wanted to see one, but I never did."

"And then the black-out came," Binkie said, "and all those brilliant lights — thousands of incandescent lights — had to be extinguished for fear enemy ships would spot our coast. Sadly, *Lumina* closed until the war was over."

He turned to Melanie and me. "Then after the war, my beguiling dance partner returned to Savannah with her family. I never saw her again until last spring."

"All's well that ends well," Ruby, the more practical of the two, said heartily.

"And if it is not well, then it is not the end," Binkie declared heartily.

They smiled happily at each other and for a second there was no one else in the room. I suspected they knew just how lucky they were to have each other to love for the rest of their lives.

"Now, Melanie, my dear, what does the doctor say about your concussion?" Aunt Ruby asked briskly.

"You'll get to question her yourself, Aunt Ruby," Melanie said. "She stops here every morning to check on me."

"My stars, that is something."

"Binkie," I said, "I've got an interesting story for you." I told him about the bones that I'd found under the antique bottles on the Boleyn estate and the interest of an ATF agent.

"Ah, the Prohibition Era," Binkie sighed, a gleam in his eyes. Binkie adores nothing more than to share his knowledge of our town's history with those who are interested.

"Prohibition in North Carolina began in 1909," he began, "ten years before the Eighteenth Amendment was ratified and became federal law. The amendment and the Volstead Act that followed prohibited the manufacture, sale, import or export of alcoholic beverages. The Bureau of Internal Revenue was charged with enforcing the law, through their revenue agents. Also there were police officers on the local level, referred to as the rum running squad, and they too enforced the law."

"The ATF agent mentioned a local officer who had been ambushed by moonshiners," I said.

"You are speaking of Leon George, who was well-thought of in this town."

Aunt Ruby reached over and placed her hand on his to

halt his speech. "Now, Binkie, these young people don't want to hear a lecture."

Melanie, who ordinarily would be fidgeting by this time and rolling her eyes heavenward, said, "Yes, we do, Aunt Ruby. Go on, Binkie."

"I'd like to hear too," I said. "I am basically ignorant when it comes to the Prohibition Era. From everything I've heard it was a romantic period. Flappers and speakeasies. Zelda and Scott Fitzgerald. Bathtub gin and bobbed hair. The Charleston." I raised my eyebrows. "Free love."

Aunt Ruby said somberly, "For every romantic notion you have about that period, I can give you one that is sobering. Free love, you say? Syphilis, I say. The disease was sexually transmitted and highly contagious. And in those times before penicillin, there was no way to treat it. People died of it or went blind. And then too, young women, some of them still in their teens, died of botched abortions."

Now Binkie patted her hand. "Now who's the lecturer, my bride?" he asked, smiling at her fondly.

"And bathtub gin," he said. "Some of those moonshiners made gin in galvanized metal tubs, such as the ones that were used for bathing and laundry. And the galvanized metal could be a problem. Often there were health risks associated with galvanized metal.

"But people loved their alcohol," he went on, and lifted his glass as if in toast. "And still do. Just as we are enjoying these cocktails now, they wanted theirs. And they were being deprived one of their pleasures. So the 'Noble Experiment' as it was called was a great failure.

"And moonshine — they also called it white lightning — wasn't at all difficult to purchase. Why, they used to sell it at a filling station at Seventh and Castle."

Aunt Ruby laughed. "And when they travelled, they'd hide it in their hot water bottles."

Binkie said, "At one point, the agents discovered five hundred pints of corn whiskey at the Atlantic Coast Line Depot, waiting to be loaded onto the train like any other goods." He threw back his head and laughed.

"And with our waterways, fine yachts, which you wouldn't suspect of being involved with rum running, would attempt to smuggle huge quantities of foreign alcohol into our ports. One was seized right out at Banks Channel.

"The rum ships would lie off the Carolina coast, then transfer their illegal cargo onto smaller vessels that would attempt to smuggle it into port. I remember reading about the case of the Albertine Adoue that was captured by the Coast Guard at Lockwoods Folly Inlet. They confiscated almost a thousand cases of bourbon, scotch, rum, brandy, even champagne. The cases were transferred to a sealed vault in the Customs House, but before they could be destroyed, eighty-eight cases had disappeared. Vanished."

Binkie chuckled. "The federal agents would pour the liquor down the sewers in the alley at the rear of the Customs House and it would run into the Cape Fear River. I suspect there were days when the alcoholic content of the river was ninety proof!"

Melanie smiled at the image.

"You mentioned Officer George," I said. "Agent Randolph told me his little dog had been shot too. That really got to me."

"Leon George was the head of our local rum running squad. A couple of years before he was killed he broke up a moonshine operation where they were using the galvanized metal tubs. Might have saved some lives. He was a popular local figure, admired and respected. Two thousand people squeezed into the church for his funeral and thousands more attended his burial."

"So what happened, Binkie? How was he killed?" Melanie asked.

"Officer George and Marshal Sam Lilly had confiscated a still in an isolated, swampy area fifteen miles northwest of Wilmington. They were driving back to Wilmington with the still when they were ambushed on a lonely stretch of road by C.W. Stewart, a moonshiner, and his son Elmer. The agents didn't even have time to reach for their guns. The car's windshield was shot out, and both men were shot repeatedly, even after they were dead. It was a vengeful killing. George's pet Airedale was in the back seat. I don't know if he was a working dog or simply a pet George like to take around with him, but even so that was no reason to kill the animal. But the Stewarts shot him too, and that helped to turn public sentiment against them.

"Leon George is buried out at Oakdale. His family had his body moved from Bellevue Cemetery to the family plot."

"Do you remember anything about a federal agent disappearing, Binkie?" I asked.

"Seems to me there was a federal agent here lending a hand about '30, '31. He went out alone one day to investigate rumors of a still and never returned to the rooming house where he was staying. Everyone suspected foul play but his body was never found so there was no proof and no suspects. And no one knew where he was going."

"He might have been the man we found," I said. "And it looks like Increase Boleyn was making moonshine."

Binkie thought for a moment, choosing his words carefully. "I'd only be speculating, but I will tell you what I know about Increase Boleyn. His ancestors had worked as mariners on the Masonboro Sound in the nineteenth century. His parents lived in Southport. They were "Sounders," people who made a living from guiding large cargo ships around the dangerous shoals that guarded the mouth of the Cape Fear River. Through thrift and hard work they accumulated the funds to purchase the small peninsula on the waterway that adjoined the property that later became Airlie. The property was conveyed to Increase Boleyn upon his father's death. Now Increase was an educated man who made wise investments, and later was granted a directorship at a local bank where he prospered. He built that lodge, and it was mighty fine. But with the crash of the stock market he, like so many others, lost his fortune.

"There were rumors that he was bootlegging and moonshining, but he was never caught. The wealthy society folks in these parts had to be buying their alcohol from someone, why not from one of their own? And he had wealthy friends who owned yachts. The yachts would tie-up at Boleyn's dock and they very well could have been transferring illegal cargo. The agents couldn't be everywhere."

"So do you think it was Boleyn who killed the agent, or ordered his death?" I asked.

Binkie gazed at me with sad eyes. "Ashley, dear, it does seem likely."

24

"I don't think I can face the inside of my house," Melanie said from the passenger seat in my Avalon. "I know I can't bear to sleep in my bedroom again. I'll picture Mickey dying there every time I go in it."

On Saturday afternoon we were parked in the driveway outside Melanie's house, and I was encouraging her to accompany me inside so she could see the work I'd done.

Her fingers strayed nervously to the crown of her hair where she'd been wounded. A hair piece now covered the shaved spot and the stitches; her hair stylist had been coming to do her hair at first. Now she was able to wash it under the shower.

We were both wearing low-rise, boot cut jeans with sweater sets, mine navy, Melanie's jade green.

"In fact," she said brightly, "I think I'll just put it on the market. This lot has appreciated tremendously in value since I bought out here. I'll make a bundle."

"But then you'd just have to spend your bundle on another house," I argued. "Waterfront property is out of sight. You of all people should know that. Okay, if that's what you decide to do, I will understand. But first let me show you what I've done before you make a decision. You said you didn't have time to see a thing that night when you got home. That you walked into the kitchen from the garage and the next thing you know you awoke in the hospital. So it's not like you have a vivid picture painted in your memory."

No, I was the one who had the vivid picture stored in my brain. The brutality of Mickey's slaying had been shocking. I'd never forget it, the way he'd been knifed so viciously. Whoever had killed him had been angry, very angry. Yet cool enough to attempt to plant the knife in Melanie's hand and make it look like she was the murderer.

I realized something then: our murderer was a complex individual.

I went around to the passenger side and opened the door for Melanie, still wanting to baby her. Taking her hand, I said, "I can't believe you are showing houses so soon. Why, you can't even stand up without feeling woozy."

"Once I'm on my feet, I'm fine," she declared. "And I can walk, Ashley. It's not like my legs were injured. It's just that I can't drive yet but the doc says maybe next week. Everyone's been so sweet, especially her. She's been dropping by your house to check on me. Can you imagine? House calls, in these days of HMOs.

"And my clients! Well, they have been steadfast and loyal, Ashley. They believe in me. They know I didn't kill anybody. Let's attend services at St. James tomorrow together. I've been skipping church too much lately and I have a lot to give thanks for."

"Sure," I said. "We'll go together, just like we always do." But I gave her face a searching look. This did not sound like Melanie. She was not generally sentimental.

"Do you know that my clients have been picking me up and doing the driving while we look at houses?" Melanie continued. "And those sweethearts, Mae Mae and Lucy Lou — well, they've been precious."

Melanie continued, "So things are working out perfectly. And I think I've found just the right situation for them. They are getting along in . . . "

"Melanie," I interrupted, "I know all that. Now let me tell you what I've done to your house. Willie has a grandson who is just starting out in the floor refinishing business so he was eager to get this job and he gave us a very good price."

Melanie arched her eye brows approvingly. She loves a bargain as much as I do. I slammed the car door shut and we started along the curving walkway to her front door. Again the day was warm and sunny, although we were nearing the end of November. Next Thursday would be Thanksgiving and we hadn't even discussed where we were spending the day or what we were going to do. Then the Saturday after Thanksgiving was the Holiday Flotilla preceded by the Festival in the Park. And we'd promised Cam that we'd be guests on his yacht, *The Hot Momma*, for the parade.

I steered Melanie up the steps to her front door. "Archie — that's Willie's grandson — ripped up and removed all the carpeting. And Melanie, your hardwood floors were in excellent condition, he simply refinished them." Melanie's ranch house dated from the seventies when it was standard practice to install hardwood floors in a new house.

I inserted the key and opened the door. "See for yourself."

We stepped inside. From the foyer we had a view in two directions, to the left into the living room and dining room, and to the right into the hallway and the bedrooms beyond. Melanie clapped her hands together and squealed with delight. "Oh, it's beautiful," she exclaimed.

Hearing those words of praise did my heart good.

"I was hoping you'd like what we did."

"You've bleached the wood, haven't you?" she asked. "And painted all the walls white. It looks so clean. And so spacious. Where's the furniture?"

"In storage and at the upholsterer's." I led the way into the living room. "I'm using that gorgeous oil painting of the sunset at Wrightsville Beach as my inspiration. Pulling the colors from it for upholstery for the furniture: the sand color of the beach, the golden-green of sea oats. With the pinks and crimsons of the sunset for throw pillows to punch up the color scheme."

We moved into the center of the room. "Those sliding glass doors are out of date, Mel. We'll replace them with French doors out to the deck. They'll look charming.

I guided her back into the foyer and down the hallway to the master bedroom. "In here, we'll have whites and creams. So clean and fresh. We're lucky to have a talented lace maker in town, Nancy Carnegie. She makes lace trimmings by hand. We have her edge white linen bedding with ecru lace."

I was hoping the purity of the color scheme would act to cleanse the decor and obliterate Melanie's memory of the violence committed here.

"It'll be beautiful, Mel. Fresh and contemporary. And if you want to sell, the refurbishing will only add to the value of the house. So what do you think?"

She grabbed me in a hug. "I think you are the most talented person in your field, Ashley Wilkes. You are special, and I take some credit for that, I had a hand in raising you. Why, I helped Mama change your diapers. And you may not remember this, but when you were very little, I spent hours coloring with you. You had a keen eye for color even then and I encouraged you to pursue art. You are the best, little sis."

I hugged her back. "I love you, Melanie. I don't know what I would have done if you hadn't recovered. I was so worried."

"I'm tough, Ashley. And so are you. Steel magnolias, that's what we are, just like Aunt Ruby."

She took a step back, holding both my hands in her own. "Ashley, this near-death experience has caused me to do a lot of thinking. I've been reviewing my life. I've made really poor choices, you know. And I intend to change all that. I've turned over a new leaf. Things are going to be different from now on. I intend to make better choices. To use my head as well as my heart. And well," she giggled, "I must confess my libido had a big influence on my choices in men.

"But poor Mickey didn't deserve what he got. You were right about him, little sis, he was trouble. Most of the men I've been involved with have been trouble. That is about to change. And I promise to be more patient with people, to try to see other points of view, and not make snap judgements."

The doorbell rang cutting off what I was going to say in response.

"Oh, shoot! Now who can that be? You expecting one of your workmen?" she asked me.

She started for the door.

"Wait, Melanie, let's see who it is before you open the door."

She turned back to me. "You're right, we have to be careful now, don't we?"

She looked out a window onto the porch. "Why, it's Crystal Lynne Boleyn. Wonder what she wants. You know, Ashley," she said in a hushed voice as if Crystal Lynne could hear through the closed door, "I never did like that girl. These days you can't tell a hottie from a hoochie, and that one is definitely a hoochie."

She held up a hand. "But I'll be nice. I promise."

She opened the door and exclaimed, "Why, Crystal Lynne, sugar, whatever are you doing here! Come right along inside, sugar. Ashley's here too. Remember her?"

"Hi, Ashley," Crystal said. "Hey, Melanie."

"Well, don't you look just like a picture," Melanie said. "Doesn't she, Ashley?"

"Gorgeous outfit, Crystal Lynne," I said.

Crystal was dressed up in a shimmery beige silk pants suit with the lace on an ivory silk camisole peeking out of the V-neck of the jacket.

Crystal reached up and brushed her hair. "I'm meeting a girlfriend for dinner," she said in a gush. "Girl talk, you know. David had to fly up to Washington. A consulting job. He still keeps a hand in."

She gazed around at the empty rooms. "You redecorating? Well, shut my mouth, 'course you are. You'd have to be, after what all . . . Melanie, sweetie, how are you feeling?"

"I'm doing fine, Crystal. Where are my manners? I'm afraid there's no place for us to sit but the bar stools in the kitchen, so let's go on back there. Can I offer you something to drink? I'm sure I've got iced tea in the fridge. And I've got wine. Which would you prefer?"

"White wine would be nice," Crystal said, setting her purse down on the kitchen counter with a thunk before sliding onto a high stool.

"Ashley, would you do the honors?" Melanie said. "Pour us all a round." She sat on the stool next to Crystal as I opened the wine cooler.

"Now what can we do for you, sugar? You didn't drive all the way out here for nothing? And, by the way, what are you doing for wheels? Y'all keep a car here?"

"Yes, we do. We have parking privileges out at the marina and so we keep a car here so we can get around town. And to take David to the airport when he flies."

She smiled at both of us. "I come with an invitation. David is flying back first thing tomorrow morning, then he's throwing a little party in the afternoon on the yacht and he especially wants the two of you to attend. We'll sail from the Wrightsville Marina at one, have a late lunch on board, and be back before dinner. And, Melanie, David said to be sure to tell you the salt air will do you a world of good. Salt air is restorative, you know."

Crystal seemed hyper, nervous, anxious to please.

"Oh, I don't know, Crystal," I said, stopping and turning away from the wine cooler, a cork screw in my hand. "She's recuperating from a head injury. She needs to take it easy."

I watched Melanie closely to gauge her reaction. Did she want to go? Or was she hoping I'd get her out of this? I knew she wasn't crazy about Crystal Lynne, and David could certainly be hard to take — a charmer one minute, a boor the next.

I'd laid the ground work for Melanie to say no. She said, "Ashley's right, shug. I know we were the dearest friends during our pageant days — best friends, actually — but you see I'm just . . . "

Crystal interrupted. "You've got to say yes, Melanie. David will be . . . well, disappointed if I don't pull this off." Her face started to get all puckery. Her lower lip trembled. "No, actually, he'll be furious. You know David, he doesn't take no for an answer. No ones knows that better than I."

And next thing I knew, Crystal Lynne was sobbing in Melanie's arms. Melanie was patting her back and making soothing sounds and casting me a helpless look over Crystal Lynne's platinum head.

Crystal Lynne lifted her face to Melanie's. "Oh, Melanie, I have made such a mess of my life. Why couldn't I have been like you? Strong. Independent. Instead I thought I couldn't make it on my own, that I needed a powerful, rich man like David to take care of me. And see where's it's gotten me. I'm miserable."

"Well, leave him," Melanie said.

"I can't. I couldn't survive."

"That's nonsense, Crystal Lynne! Of course, you can survive. Survive and prosper. Look at Ashley and me. We'll help you, won't we, Ashley?"

I looked at her, my mouth dropping open, not knowing what to say.

Crystal Lynne pulled back and stared at us. "If I leave him, I'll get nothing. All these years of living with that egomaniac and putting up with his foul moods, his cruelty, his temper, and I'll get nothing. I'll be out in the cold, and he'll still have that gorgeous yacht and the hunting lodge you're restoring for him, Ashley. And it will be beautiful, I know it will. But I'm locked in to a pre-nup. My granny Lynne always said I was a foolish girl, and I've proven her right."

She started to sob again.

Melanie dragged over the box of Kleenex and handed her a wad of tissues. "Dry your eyes, Crystal Lynne. We'll think of something, honey bunch."

Crystal Lynne swiped at her eyes and said, "There's got to be a better way. You see, I've fallen in love. With a much younger man. Oh, he's everything my heart desires. We've got to find a way to be together."

She narrowed her eyes, considering, wondering if she should utter her next confession. She decided to. "You see, I know things about David. Things that could ruin him. He has bribed congressmen. I could bring them all down if I told what I know. There'd be a huge scandal."

She dabbed at her eyes and seemed to brighten. "We're going to find a way. He'll help me." He meaning the new man in her life.

She picked up her purse and turned to leave. "Say you'll come, Melanie. Tomorrow at one. The Wrightsville Marina."

She paused at the door. "I'll tell David you'll be there when he phones."

Melanie gave me a helpless look and a shrug. "Okay," she said. "We'll be there."

"Oh, thanks, sweetie," she said, and hugged Melanie again. "You are the best. I've always admired you so much. Wish I could be just like you."

Then she was gone. And I was confused.

25

Later that night, Jon and I had an old-fashioned Saturday night date. I brushed out my hair which is getting long, slipped into a dress, and when I came downstairs, Melanie clapped, Cam whistled, and Binkie and Aunt Ruby beamed their approval.

"She doesn't wear dresses often enough," Melanie said.

"But when she does — va, va, va, voom!" Cam laughed.

Jon arrived promptly at eight, dressed in a handsome dark suit and smelling of cologne and roses. "Hello, gorgeous," he said, his customary greeting for me, but this time he said it with awe, as if holding his breath. And that is exactly what he told me next. "You take my breath away."

He held his hands behind his back, grinning and waiting, until I said, "What are you hiding?" But the fragrance gave his surprise away.

At that point he swung his right arm forward dramatically to present me with a huge bouquet of red roses, at least a dozen and a half.

"Oh, Jon, they're beautiful!" I exclaimed, accepting them. "Thank you." I brushed his lips with mine.

Aunt Ruby, who had followed me into the reception hall, said, "I'll just take those and put them in water for you, Ashley, darling." She buried her face in the roses. "My stars, don't they smell divine. Now, you young people run along and have fun."

But Cam and Melanie, and Binkie too, had to say hello first, to hug and shake hands with Jon. I saw then how much more warmly they greeted Jon than they had ever greeted Nick. Your family and friends know what is best for you, I suddenly realized, often times better than you know yourself.

We got into Jon's Escalade, Jon holding the door for me. How many times had I ridden in that car with him? Traveling to work sites, driving to and from countless lunches and dinners. Once we'd even gone out shagging — a quasi date — but never a real, formal date until tonight. I had to admit to feeling just a little bit shy.

But, I told myself, it's Jon. Dear Jon. I knew him almost as well as I knew myself. Yet, he was capable of surprising me, as he had with his ability to kiss. He was a good lover, thoughtful and slow. But there was more to loving than technique. Ours was good because we never ran out of words; we always had so much to tell each other. And many private jokes to share; a kind of verbal shorthand when we spoke. Life was good for me right now.

If it weren't for Melanie and the trouble she was in, I'd be floating on Cloud Nine. As Jon took Nun to Front Street and drove north, I told him about how Crystal Lynne had coerced Melanie and me into accepting David Boleyn's invitation to attend a party on his yacht for the next afternoon.

"She implied that he'd make her life miserable if she didn't get Melanie and me to agree to come. What does it matter to him if we're there or not? It's not like we're friends with the man!"

Jon said, "I got a call this afternoon from some flunky

who works for David. He told me I was expected to put in an appearance — command performance — something like that, on the yacht tomorrow. I assume it will be work related, that David wants to review the renovations we've made. Cam's coming too."

"Well, then with you two there, it will be tolerable. But that Crystal Lynne, she's a mess."

"Don't sweat it, Ashley. We can stand them for a few hours. We don't have any choice, when you get right down to it. He's our client. If it's not a meeting on his yacht, it will be somewhere else. We can't avoid the man. We just have to put up with his eccentric behavior and see the job through."

"You are right, as usual, Jon," I said and rested my hand lightly on his thigh.

"Now can we talk about something more interesting?" he asked with a smile in his voice. "Like us." He glanced over at me and I saw his face take on that special glow it gets when his eyes meet mine.

"Okay. Where are we going?" I asked.

"A surprise, but we're almost there, so you'll know soon enough."

He pulled into a parking space on Front Street near Princess. "Oh, you're taking me to Prima. This is perfect. It's so romantic there."

"Just what I had in mind," Jon said and got out of the driver's side.

I started to open the door for myself, then stopped. Let him, I thought. He gets a kick out of performing these little demonstrations of love for me. And I liked it too. I was so used to getting down into the trenches with the men on the job site that it was nice to be treated like and feel like a lady now and again.

Prima is a relaxing Bistro with a romantic edge. The tables are round with cane chairs drawn up; large canvases with bold colors in oil covered the walls. I sipped water from a cobalt blue water goblet, my mouth suddenly dry as I realized how much my life had changed. Sometimes things work out better than you expect. I hoped that would be true when Melanie's troubles were resolved.

I studied the wine list. "I think I'll have the Valpolicella," I told Jon. "I decided the minute I hit the door to have steak. I eat so much fish and sometimes a girl just needs red meat."

"You order whatever your heart desires," Jon said. "The Valpolicella sounds good to me too. Should I order a bottle?"

I reached across the table and touched his hand. "Not for me, thanks. One glass will be enough. I don't want to ruin this special evening by getting looped."

"Well, I'm driving so one glass is all I want too. We'll have champagne later," he said mysteriously.

"Oh, is someone planning a party?" I asked.

His eyes twinkled merrily. He was so happy. Oh, dear God, I breathed, please let him stay this way.

"Actually, someone is planning a very private party," he said and grinned.

"Oh? And are you going to tell me about it?"

"When the time comes. Patience, little one. Now here's our waiter. What is your pleasure?"

I ordered the filet mignon. It came with a wild mushroom demi-glace. "Good choice," the waiter said. Jon told him he'd have a ribeye, medium rare. The waiter collected our menus and quietly departed.

A couple being seated a few tables away caught my eye and I dragged my gaze away from Jon's loving eyes. The woman's blonde head was familiar and I recognized her instantly. I studied her and her partner.

"What?" Jon asked, turning where I was looking.

"Remember I was just telling you about our bizarre conversation with Crystal Lynne earlier today? Well, there she is. And look who she's with. I don't believe it. Ali Shariff. Now what . . . ? Oh no, you don't suppose he's her new love interest? He's so homely."

"Now, Ashley, don't you think that's a superficial judgement? You don't really know the guy. He could be a great fellow," Jon said tenderly.

"You're right. I shouldn't make snap judgements."

When our waiter came with our wine, I took another opportunity to study Crystal and Ali. She had on the same shimmery beige suit she'd worn to Melanie's house. So Ali was the girlfriend she was meeting.

And Ali, I had to admit as I watched him stare at Crystal, was transformed. His fierce expression had vanished. His face had softened, glowed in the way Jon's face glowed when he saw mine.

So he's in love with her, I thought. He must be the younger man she told us she'd fallen for. I thought of David Boleyn and the propriety manner in which he treated Crystal, as if she were a piece of meat he was about to devour, or a pet he owned.

"They're in love, Jon," I whispered.

He turned his head to give them a good look. They were so wrapped up in each other, they didn't see us. They weren't aware of anyone else in the room.

"Well, good for them!" Jon told me. "In this mad and dangerous world, you're a fool if you don't take love where you find it."

"You're so smart," I said, and gave him a big smile, so proud of him and his wisdom.

"I know a place that plays romantic music so we can dance. And there's champagne on ice," he said, bending toward me as we stepped out into the soft night.

"I'm all for that," I said. "But I can't wait." I wrapped my arms around his waist and gave him a long kiss.

We drove to Wrightsville Beach holding hands, to Jon's house on the waterway side of the island. Out here a wind was blowing in from the ocean, a warm moist wind fed by the Gulf Stream.

I've always liked the way Jon's house backed up to the marshes, always felt at home there. He had outfitted it with an eye for comfort.

We danced on the polished living room floor to a CD that had been recorded just for lovers. "I love the way Rod Stewart sings those old standards," I said. Stewart was singing "It Had to be You" in that gravely voice of his.

Jon sang softly in my ear, the words of the song just for me, for us.

And then the CD changed, and Etta James big throaty voice came of out the speakers singing, "At Last, My Love Has Come Along."

Well, I was thrilled. I love that song. We held each other, moving very slowly, and sang with her.

The music went on to something soft. Time for a change of venue.

"You promised champagne," I whispered. "Where is it?"

"In the bedroom," he replied, his voice husky in my ear. "For later. Can't you wait?"

"No darling, I cannot wait another minute."

"Just can't get enough of me, can you?" he said, lifting me off my feet and carrying me down a hallway to the bedroom. Candles twinkled softly and a bottle of champagne was set in an ice bucket. There were many pillows on the bed, and a plump comforter already turned down.

"But we won't be able to dance in here," Jon teased. "Bed takes up too much floor space."

I nuzzled his warm neck. He smelled of aftershave and his

natural smell, and uncannily of sunshine. "We could dance lying down," I murmured. "I've heard that's fun too."

26

David Boleyn met us at the gangway and welcomed us into the salon. He was in an expansive mood, cheerful and hearty. Playing to his captive audience, no doubt.

"Let me show you around," he said, after kissing both me and Melanie on the cheek.

I caught Melanie's eye over his shoulder. Her face wore the same puzzled expression as mine must have. What gives? we were thinking.

With a friendly hand on Jon's shoulder, David pointed out the upper deck arrangement. "Wet bar over there. Help yourself to anything you want, although Crystal's got a spread fit for royalty up on the flybridge.

"Over there on the port side is the galley. Beyond that is the day head." He turned to Melanie and me. "Otherwise known to you girls as the 'powder room'. Up in the bow is the pilothouse but we'll be piloting from the flybridge today."

To Cam and Jon he said, "The flybridge has an upper navigation station, electronics suite, touch screen PC monitoring system — the whole shebang."

In David's world, women would not be expected to know

about such things as a Northstar GPS/plotter. David had a lot to learn about women.

"And behind you there is the aft deck," he indicated.

I looked through curved sliding glass doors to the aft deck where two flags — the American flag and the Confederate flag — fluttered in the breeze off Motts Channel.

I turned my attention to the interior decor. Lush. Tasteful. The compartments and the paneling were made of African mahogany laminates. There were a sofa and club chairs, an oval dining table that seated six with a mirrored headliner centered above.

We moved past the galley and up a few steps into the pilothouse, made a sharp left and took the stairway to the flybridge where the other guests were having drinks. Here, in the open flybridge, we would party under a sunny and cloudless sky, while the black and silent waters of the Intracoastal Waterway ferried us south.

With David and Cam at the helm talking mariner's talk, we cruised out of Wrightsville Marina, south past Bradley Creek, and into the waterway.

You could have knocked me over with a feather when I saw who the other guests were. But I worked the room, or worked the flybridge to be correct, shook hands and said hello nicely. You have to give Mama credit for teaching her girls good manners — under the most trying of circumstances.

Of course I was pleased if not a bit surprised to see Walt Brice there. "I didn't know you knew David," I said.

"Oh, Dave and I go way back," he replied, giving me a light hug. Walt was a bachelor; no female companion accompanied him.

Brie Bitterman sat huddled between her parents in the corner of an elevated white vinyl L-shaped settee, looking like she'd rather be in a dentist's chair. How had David managed to drag her on board? On the stage she exuded presence, but in social situations she was as sulky and withdrawn as any resentful teenager.

I said hello to her and to Clay and Bunny Bitterman. They weren't exactly pleased to see me or Melanie.

David got up and left Cam at the helm to pilot the ship and Cam seemed overjoyed to be piloting this top-of-the-line watercraft. Jon slipped into the empty helm chair and chatted with him as we navigated past Hewletts Creek on the starboard side.

With one arm around my shoulder and the other arm around Melanie's, David turned us to face the Bittermans. "Now, I love all you guys. And I want my friends to be friends with each other. So as a personal favor to me, kiss and make-up, folks."

Melanie squirmed out from under his beefy arm. *Don't manhandle me*, her attitude clearly said. David did not take offense.

Speaking directly to Clay, David said, "Melanie Wilkes is the best darn realtor this town has ever seen and I want you to give her back the listing on your house that you took away from her. She no more killed Joey Fielding than I did. Am I right, Walt?"

"You are right, David, and the police are coming around to seeing it our way. Joey Fielding was into things that should have aroused their suspicions. And with a word from me into the right ear at the D.A.'s office, they are looking into that right now. I fully expect the charges to be dropped soon. Very soon."

Melanie fairly did a tap dance, and would have except that dancing might have set off a headache. "Oh, Walt, what good news? Did you hear that, sweetheart?" she called to Cam who let out a cheer and pumped the air with his fist.

Walt looked grim. "I won't rest until they drop the charges and Melanie's good name is restored to her."

"My clients are sticking by me," Melanie told everyone. "They are loyal and supportive and I love 'em to death." She brushed a sentimental tear from her eyelash.

Melanie? Sentimental? She *had* turned over a new leaf. I gave her a hug.

"Well, why was she always hanging around Joey all summer, every time I called?" sulky Brie wanted to know, talking about Melanie like she wasn't there.

Melanie's eyes narrowed into dangerous slits and I was afraid she might tell moody Brie where to do and what to do when she got there — new leaf or no new leaf — but she must have instantly considered that the listing of a multi-million dollar waterfront property was at stake.

She smiled. And Melanie's megawatt smile could light up a dark cave. "Brie, sugar," she said sweetly, leaning forward to place a hand on Brie's bare knee, "I told you. I was helping Joey acquire that property for his restaurant. And helping him find the best people to renovate it. Just doin' my job, sugah, same as I'll do a bang-up job for your folks." She included Bunny and Clay in her dazzling smile.

Clay cleaned his throat with a hrrumph. "Guess I was a mite hasty there, Melanie, jumped to conclusions. The wrong conclusions." He stretched out his hand. "Friends?"

Melanie took his hand and shook it. "Friends!" she said warmly.

"You've got the listing back. We'll take care of the paperwork tomorrow. Okay?"

"Perfect," Melanie responded. She leaned into Bunny and gave her a little hug. "Let's do lunch, sweetie. On me. We'll go downtown. Try something new. Let me look at my schedule and I'll give you a buzz. Okay?"

"Sure," Bunny said. "I always thought the world of your mama and daddy. You, too, Melanie."

Walt stood up and slapped David on the back, the two of

them just about the same size, tall, burly. "Well, you done it, you old scalawag. We ought to dominate you for a Nobel Peace Prize. You're as smooth as old Jimmy Carter any day."

Walt grinned at David, then he went to the wet bar and fixed himself another drink.

And where was our hostess, Crystal Lynne, while all these warm and fuzzies were taking place? Out on the bridge deck in shorts and a halter, soaking up the sun and chatting up Ali Shariff.

I went out on the pretext of greeting my hostess but really to satisfy my curiosity, remembering how I had seen them together just last night. They'd been lost in each other.

They were stretched out side by side on two lounges, speaking in undertones. Was David blind? Didn't he care? Or would she pay later?

Ali had on shorts and had removed his shirt. He had a lot of dark hair on his chest and legs and I could only think that you'd have to change the sheets every morning or else use a velcro brush to mop the hair out of the bed. But some women like that sort of overt masculinity.

I flashed back to Jon's long, lean body next to mine last night. Some blonde hair sure, but not this grizzly bear's pelt.

I said "hey," flashed them a smile that was fueled by my memories of my night with Jon and not by the sight of them, and returned to the flybridge. A sumptuous feast was spread on a large pedestal table that was mounted to the deck. I scooped up a shrimp with my fingers, dipped it in red cocktail sauce and popped it into my mouth.

We had already passed Whiskey Creek and were heading for Carolina Beach.

David, who had been engaged in a quiet conversation with Walt, noted our location, and headed for the helm. "Let me take over here," he said to Cam. Jon gave up the helm chair but remained standing near by, eyes rivetted on the water ahead.

Walt brushed by me and made for the stairs.

David said, "We're about to sail into Snow's Cut and the current there can be tricky. It's swift so you've got to know what you're doing."

We passed through the cut, the water a bit rough, then sailed out into the mighty Cape Fear which was rushing head-long to the ocean.

I reached for another shrimp, swallowed it, and suddenly didn't feel too good. The horizon seemed to be tilting, like it was listing from side to side. And under my feet the deck seemed to sway.

There wasn't time to speak or to call to Jon for help. I clamped a hand over my mouth and ran for the stairs and the day head.

Would I make it? Seasick! I was seasick! I'd never been seasick in my life and I had sailed often.

I reached the day head, pushed on the door, but it was locked.

Down the stairs to the lower deck, I thought. I'd find a head there.

I ran along the lower deck companionway toward the bow, holding my mouth closed with my hand, trying to con-trol the waves of nausea that were wrenching at my insides.

I threw open the first door I came to. Boxes. A state-room, clearly, but filled with boxes and no way around them. Crystal's decorating project.

I flung open the next door. The same.

Running back the way I'd come, I pushed open a bi-fold door and raced into the master stateroom. Darted through it and into the master head. Where I found relief.

When the nausea subsided, I stood up and ran water in the sink. Washed my face, found a paper cup and rinsed my mouth. Looked at my reflection in the mirror over the gran-ite countertop. I opened one of the mahogany compartments and found a bottle of mouthwash, splashed some into the paper cup and rinsed my mouth again.

In the mirror, my face looked pale, my eyes huge. But at least I felt better. I dried my hands, cut through the stateroom, and went out into the companionway. Where I encountered a glowering David Boleyn.

His arms were crossed over his barrel chest. He gave me a narrow grimace. "You get lost? Thought I showed you where the little girls room was," he said.

Well shoot, what had happened to our gracious host? Where had he misplaced the charm? And why?

"I wasn't feeling well," I said defensively, although why I should feel defensive I didn't know — it wasn't like I was stealing Crystal's jewelry. "Walt was in the day head."

He stood back to let me pass before him and followed me to stairway.

"It's not like I had a choice," I said. "Didn't know this was off limits."

I was mad. I didn't feel good, and this jerk was making me feel worse.

Suddenly he was jovial again. He ran a hand around my waist. "Sorry, Ashley. It's just that those are our private quarters and Crystal doesn't like anybody messing around in her private bathroom. And she's redecorating the other three staterooms and she doesn't like anybody to see the mess. Come on back up and I'll fix you a Bloody Mary that'll fix that stomach of yours right quick."

The man was mercurial. No wonder Crystal preferred Ali. At least he was consistently sullen.

27

Back on the flybridge I found everyone filling plates from the buffet. I saw Jon's concerned face and hastened to assure him I was all right.

Crystal had provided a spread of cold salmon and lobster, shrimp, dips, salsa, chips, and a large fresh fruit platter. Plus any kind of alcoholic beverage you could think of. We would surely not be wanting dinner later.

While I'd been fighting nausea on the lower deck, Cam had sailed us past Kure Beach and Ft. Fisher. The quaint village of Southport lay to starboard. In the distance, on the port side, Bald Head Island seemed to float on the water. As we drew near, I saw the marina and the ships chandlery where colorful flags flapped in the wind."

At that point the river bore us along toward the Atlantic and the infamous Frying Pan Shoals. "She's more than sea worthy," David said, "but we'll turn back here."

Looking at me, he said, "You're feeling better now, aren't you, Ashley? Don't look so peaked. That Bloody Mary of mine will fix what ails you, whether it be a hangover or heart break."

With that, he fixed Crystal with an accusing glare, a glare that fairly shouted, I've got your number, sister.

"I am feeling better," I confessed. "There's Old Baldy!" I pointed and we all turned for a view of the massive stone lighthouse that stood guard over Bald Head Island and the entrance to the Cape Fear.

"There's a ghost story associated with that island," I said. The Bloody Mary had loosened my tongue.

"Ashley and her ghost stories," Melanie said with a wicked grin. Melanie had on a cute ball cap. It covered the stitches on the back on her head, but with her long auburn hair pulled through the cap's hole, no one would suspect she didn't have a full head of hair under it.

"The ghost story is called 'The haunting of Theodosia Burr,'" I continued, ignoring her. Someone had to rescue this sorry excuse for a party.

"Well, let's hear it," Cam said.

"Growing up around here, I know it, of course, but you go ahead and tell the others," David said, casting a sharp eye at Ali. "Ali wouldn't have heard it. He grew up in some donkey pasture in the Middle East." His voice was bitter with contempt.

"Who was Theodosia Burr?" Cam asked. "A relative of Aaron Burr?"

"His daughter," I replied. "And the wife of the governor of South Carolina. In 1812 she sailed out of Georgetown on her way to New York to meet her father. Pirates attacked her ship off the North Carolina coast. There are two versions of the story. One is that she and her crew were forced to walk the plank. The other version is that she was held captive by the pirates on Smith Island — that's what Bald Head Island used to be called. In her desperation to escape from them, she ran into the ocean and drowned herself.

"To this day, she haunts the beaches of Bald Head Island,

wearing a long flowing gown. Those who've witnessed her say you can see right through her, and that she vanishes as mysteriously as she appears."

"Oh pish-posh," Melanie said. "Probably a woman in her nightie out looking for her dog."

Everyone laughed and some of the tension was relieved.

In the middle of my story, appearing bored and behaving with ill-mannered rudeness, Brie had taken her loaded buffet plate out onto the bridge deck. Now Ali followed her and cornered her, remonstrated with her about something — his voice volatile, his hands waving wildly as he talked. But Brie was having none of it. She shook her head vehemently, her long hair flying. Then she gave him a shove with her free hand and slipped by him to rejoin her parents. She and Clay huddled in a mumbled conversation.

Everyone had seen the confrontation. But we were all trying to make the best of a bad afternoon.

"The view from up here is marvelous," I said, aiming for cheerfulness. "Our daddy used to take us sailing when he was alive. You can't live out on the waterway and not sail."

"You grew up near the water?" David asked.

"Yes. We lived on Summer Rest Road while my dad was alive. My mama lived in the same house until she moved to her family's home in Savannah with her sister."

If I could keep chattering, maybe the fighting would stop. So I babbled. "When I was a little girl I used to think that the ICW was a natural body of water, like the ocean or the Cape Fear. But it's man made. The Army Corps of Engineers dredged it back in the twenties and thirties. They connected the natural sounds and inlets by carving through the land and opening a twelve foot deep channel that runs to Key West."

"Actually, it was begun long before that, Ashley," Walt, who was something of a history buff, gently corrected me.

"The ICW has its roots in the Dismal Swamp as long ago as 1784. Slave labor built a twenty-two mile canal to Norfolk. They dug it by hand. The cotton growers needed a waterway to ship their cotton to Norfolk so they could export it. Then Congress got involved in the early nineteen hundreds and decreed we needed a commercial waterway for our economy."

"Clouds movin' in," David said from the helm. "Cold front from Canada coming in tonight. Jon, you want to take the wheel for a while. I'm gonna help myself to another plate of Crystal's victuals."

Ahead of us, the state ferry crossed the Cape Fear on its journey from Ft. Fisher to Southport.

David moved from the helm to stand near Bunny and Clay at the buffet. "You know the Army Corps practically built that island you live on. It used to be a little bitty spit of land, known as the Hammocks, not much there. The Army Corps piled up the sand and mud they'd dredged from the sound onto the island and expanded it."

His face darkened. "They also chopped off a big piece of my granddaddy's peninsula. You think the big bad government ever paid us for that land? No-sirree-bob!"

Finally Ali, who had not spoken except to Crystal and Brie, joined the conversation, maybe wanting to show up David. "The state is going to build a huge commercial port right about there," he said, waving an arm to indicate the shore north of Southport. They have already acquired the land. Say it will provide many jobs. But no one's saying how it will impact recreational sailing."

David exploded. Ali had evidently prodded his last nerve. "Well, sure we need another port. That's because this crippled nation of ours doesn't manufacture or export a dang thing any more. All we do is import goods from China, so sure we need another port to receive all those Chinese container ships with their cheap and shoddy goods!"

His face grew red and he turned to the helm. "Look folks, it's getting chilly up here. So why don't y'all go on down to the salon where it's warm. I'll bring her into port myself."

When Cam offered to keep him company at the helm, he blurted, "Don't need no help."

It was already dark when we docked at the Wrightsville Marina. David came down from the flybridge and stood at the gangway to bid us each a goodbye. He and Crystal had some-how miraculously settled their differences because they stood together, arms entwined, the picture of the perfect host and hostess.

As I said goodbye, I added to Crystal, "I saw all your boxes on the lower deck. David told me about your decorat-ing project. Please let me know if I can help. I'll be glad to give you advice, one friend to another."

"Thanks, Ashley, I may take you up on that."

"No, you won't," David said firmly. "You got plenty of talent yourself. You don't need no help. Thank you girls for coming. You have yourself a nice night, you hear."

As Melanie and I hurried down the gangplank she said in my ear, "Well, that was surely the cruise from hell, not to be confused with the social event of the year. More like a party to die for. Die from boredom and tedium. You could cut the hostility with a knife."

"Crystal has got to get out of that marriage," I said. "That man is a time bomb ready to explode. I can't believe how Ali and Crystal flaunt their relationship right in front of him. Oh, I can't wait till this project is finished so I never have to see either one of them again."

"So then, why did you offer to help her with her decorat-ing?" Melanie accused.

"You're right. Why did I? I feel sorry for her. And also because I'm used to being a nice 'little girl.'"

"Speaking of girl, I hate the way he calls us 'the girls,'"

Melanie hissed. "The way he says it so demeaning. You never hear him call Cam and Jon and Walt 'the boys,' do you?"

Cam and Jon had preceded us down the gangplank and waited on the boardwalk.

"There are 'the boys' now," I said happily and walked into Jon's arms.

"What are y'all talking about?" Cam asked.

Melanie laced her arms around his waist and kissed his chin. "Oh nothing, sugar, just how handsome you are." Turning to me and Jon with a grin, she said, "Did you hear that? My California 'boy' just said his first y'all."

28

Monday morning dawned seasonably chilly for late November. The air was clear, the sky was blue with little white clouds scudding along from inland. But by noon the sun had warmed the air as it so often does here on the coast. And because I had grown accustomed to my daily constitutional, I was eager to walk. Already my slacks and jeans were fitting better — not tugging in the wrong places — and I felt sleeker. My job is surely more active than a desk job but I don't get much exercise; a lot of what I do is stand around and tell others what to do. It's not like I am the one who climbs a ladder to the roof.

Jon was working from home today. His presence is not always required on the site; neither is mine. So I slipped out to my van where I ate a carton of fat free peach yogurt. I patted my mouth with a tissue then pulled down the sun visor to check my face in the mirror. There were dirt smears on my forehead and I wiped them off.

My dark brown hair looked a little wilder than it normally does because of the stiff breezes. I pulled a cobweb off a curl, then combed my hair. I freshened my lipstick, and blinked at myself in the mirror. My eyes are gray, but in a certain light they look violet. Jon says they are periwinkle and that periwinkle is his favorite color.

I drove the short jaunt to Airlie Gardens and went in the back way. The gardeners were taking their lunch break too and we waved as I walked by. I had become a familiar figure to them, and knew some of them by name.

I hit the walking trail at a fast pace. I had the whole park to myself —all 67 acres — because the gardens are closed to the public during the winter months. Every once in a while an icy blast blew in from the west so I pulled the hood of my sweat jacket up over my head. But as I walked briskly, revving up to long strides, I grew warm and unzipped my jacket.

I passed the stables and took the Bradley Creek overlook for a short stretch. Then I turned inland onto the driveway and headed toward the Airlie oak tree which is reported to be anywhere from four hundred to eight hundred years old. Spanish Moss hung from its ancient branches and Resurrection Fern appeared among the leaves here and there.

I got on the walking trail and walked through the Showcase Gardens that circled around the lake where white swans glided on the water. Mrs. Pembroke had dammed a salt-water lagoon to create a large artificial lake. The lake and the swans reminded me of Italy and how I'd discovered the depth of my feelings for Jon there.

I'm happy with him, I told myself. With him, I experienced none of the acute anxiety I used to feel with Nick, wondering if and when he'd come home, wondering just where I ranked on his list of priorities. With Jon I came first, and rather than that knowledge causing me take him for granted, it made me value him more. I could relax into this love affair, I didn't have to worry needlessly. I was secure. A girl really grows up between the ages of twenty-four and twenty-six, I realized.

The tops of the trees swayed in the wind, the branches creaking. A sharp crack sounded. The breaking of a branch? It sounded more like someone had stepped on a dry twig. Was someone else out walking too? I glanced back over my shoulder but the path was empty.

I maintained my brisk stride and hurried along the path among immense azalea bushes that were taller than I was. In April they would be in full bloom — red and pink and white — dazzling because there were hundreds of thousands of them.

Sarah Pembroke had created these gardens in the early years of the nineteen-hundreds. The gardens had reached their peak in the late 1920s with a half million azaleas and five thousand camellias. People came from Boston and New York to view her gardens, and to attend private concerts by famous singers like the Great Caruso.

Those days too had been the peak of Prohibition. What a different world it had been then. Wilmington had been nothing like it was today. The Boleyn lodge was nearby and we had proof that illegal alcohol had been distilled there in large quantities. In those days, at social gatherings a flask was passed around so everyone could get a snort of illegal whiskey, and most times the punch bowl would be spiked. The entire era had fostered a sense of lawlessness, a disregard for law and order. People died of whiskey poisoning. Law men were shot while enforcing the law of the nation.

Thank goodness that unpopular, unenforceable amendment had been repealed. The same thing would happen today if the government ever decided to prohibit cigarettes. They would become more popular than ever.

I looked up at tall cedar trees and was reminded of an amusing story about Sarah Pembroke that made me smile to myself. She had gone on a tour of the Greek islands where she discovered a beautiful tree. She carefully planted the tree in a tub, tended it, and had porters drag it around for the remainder of her tour. Then she transported it all the way home to Airlie. Smile. Where she discovered it was identical to the sea cedars that grew here in her very own garden.

Behind me I felt a turbulence of air and heard the whoosh sound of sudden motion. My defense mechanisms knew what it signified before my brain registered what was happening. The hair on the back of my neck stood up on full alert and my adrenalin started to pump. Fight or flight!

I whirled around just as someone swung a stout limb at my head. I had an impression of a man in black before I threw myself to the ground. At the same time someone else was yelling my name and I heard the footfalls of my attacker as he ran away.

"Ashley! Are you all right?"

I looked up and saw Ali Shariff crouching next to me.

"I'm okay," I said. "I skinned my knees I think."

He stood up and leaned over me. "Here, let me help you up." He took my arm and assisted me to my feet.

I brushed off my jeans. They were ripped at the knees.

"Can you walk?" he asked.

I took a few faltering steps, forcing my knees to work. "Yes, I can walk. Nothing broken," I said. "Did you see him?" I asked. "He was going to hit me with that branch."

"I saw him sneak up behind you with that limb and lift it to strike you. I shouted your name."

I stopped and looked into his face. "Thank you. You saved me from an attacker. Did you recognize him?"

"I did not recognize him. He was large, I know that. He was dressed in black and had the hood of his wind breaker pulled far forward on his face. I could not see his face. I'm sorry." And he did seem to be genuinely sorry.

"Well, what are you doing here? The park is officially closed. The garden crew know me so they let walk here. You weren't following me, were you?"

Ali sighed noisily, and avoided my eyes. "Yes, I was following you. I parked my car in a driveway across Airlie Road and walked through the undergrowth."

"But why! What do you want from me?" I was upset. My knees were hurting, and my hip. Someone had tried to attack me. And Ali was admitting he'd been following me. Then I realized that his presence might have saved me from being injured, or even killed. Obviously, he meant me no harm.

He said, "I am most sorry, Ashley, but I need to talk to you. Face to face. I thought if I called, you might hang up on me. Crystal said you were kind. That you might help me. Your sister hired a private investigator to check everyone's alibis, I know that much. I want to know where Brie was that day. Who she was meeting with. She is going to fire me, after all I've done for her."

He stretched out his open palms, pleading. "She will end my career. I want to know who has lured her away from me! What they are offering her so I can counter offer. So can you tell me that? What did the investigator learn? Who did she and her father meet with in Charlotte the day Joey Fielding was killed?"

Poor Ali. How awful for him. "I honestly don't know, Ali. I never heard. If it's in the report, I never heard about it. I don't think the investigator ever discovered who she met with, just that she was in Charlotte that day. Now it's my turn to be sorry."

By then we had reached the maintenance buildings and my van. "I'll drive you to your car," I said. I started to open the driver's side door when one of the gardeners waved, called for me to wait, and hurried toward us.

"Miss Ashley, there was a man looking for you," the gardener said. "I told him you were walking in the park. I thought it was okay. He was an officer of the law. He showed me a large shiny badge. ATF, he said."

Then he noticed the grime on my face, my torn and dirty jeans, and his face crumpled with concern. "Are you all right, Miss Ashley? Did you fall?"

29

"I'm making a sweet potato casserole and Aunt Ruby is making chestnut stuffing. We've already bought a smoked turkey breast from a specialty food store. You can make the salad, baby sister," Melanie said. "We'll eat right after the games are over. I've got some of those huge mums and we'll decorate your dining room in the morning."

She was wearing a pair of superbly fitted low-rise slacks in chocolate brown, a nutmeg sweater set, brown suede boots with kitten heels. My sister can put together a coordinated outfit blindfolded. And she had her hair piece on; the color was so uniform you couldn't tell it was not her own hair.

The stitches from her head wound had been removed, her driving privileges had been restored, and for the moment she was driving sanely. How long would that last? How long would this new leaf last? I asked myself. Melanie making sweet potato casserole! Indeed! Melanie doesn't cook any more than I do. We both think restaurants and take-out are the best inventions of modern society.

"Now where are we going?" I asked from the passenger seat. "You said this was urgent."

But she went on describing the menu, "Jon is bringing the wine. And Cam is bringing dessert. Pecan pie and pumpkin pie. I'm so excited; I organized everything. We'll be like a family again." She started to give me a light punch on the arm, then checked herself.

"Can you believe it? The man can bake. A regular pastry chef! I'm so lucky."

"That *is* good news," I said sarcastically. "We need a cook in the family. You, Jon and I are as helpless in the kitchen as Binkie is. If it weren't for other people's cooking we'd starve to death."

Now why was I feeling sulky? I was acting more like Brie Bitterman than my own sunny self.

I chalked up my mood to the skepticism the police had shown when they'd "investigated" my "alleged" attack on Monday. They took my statement, went with me to Airlie Gardens, but we never could find the branch or any clues. They seemed unimpressed with my story and thought they were doing their job when they warned me not to walk in isolated places.

The gardners confirmed that I'd entered the park alone. They had not seen Ali go into the park, but they told the police that he had returned with me to my car after I'd been attacked. Excitedly, they'd told them all about the agent who'd flashed a big silver badge. They couldn't describe him except to say that he was tall and husky, had on a black wind breaker with a hood. He had arrived on foot. They had seen him go into the park but never saw him leave.

And by then, Ali Shariff was gone and I didn't have his number, although the police said they'd find him and talk to him. See if he could confirm my story, was what they meant but didn't say.

"How are your knees?" Melanie asked. "Are they healing okay?"

"Forming some little scabs. I feel like I'm about five with skinned knees."

The young doctor I had seen at one of those "Doc in the Box" places had been more professional than the cops. He cleaned my scraped knees and elbow, agreed that we didn't need X rays, said I'd be fine, and asked me out on a date. "I make house calls," he had said, and grinned.

I had to laugh. He was cute. I said no thanks but that I'd be sure not to let any one else tend my scraped knees in the future. Why is it a woman who is taken is more attractive to a man than a woman who is available? And they seem to be able to sense when you are not available. Dr. Phil says that with men the old adage, "The grass is always greener on the other side of the fence," is true. Men want what they cannot have. The fair doctor and I parted friends.

"So where are we going?" I asked Melanie.

She mumbled something.

"What?"

"Joey's apartment," she said, voice shrill, daring me to contradict her.

Which I did after I shook my head and cleared my ears. "Did you say 'Joey's apartment?' What are you talking about? We can't go there. He's dead, Melanie! What are you thinking of? Breaking into his apartment?" So that's why we were driving down South College Road toward Monkey Junction. Oh, no! Not this again. This is precisely what had started all our troubles.

Well, if truth be told, I have done a little B&E in my lifetime but only when there was something very vital — life and death — at stake. There was no life involved in this situation any more. The man was dead.

Melanie looked at me. "Watch the road," I said. I had that one memorized. Why did I let her drive? Why didn't I just insist on being the driver when we were out on one of her covert operations?

"Walt said Joey was into suspicious goings on that no one knew anything about. Remember him saying that?" Melanie asked.

"Yes, I do. He made that statement on Sunday on The Cruise from Hell. Let's not talk about that experience, I'm trying to forget it."

"Well, I figured, if we could get into Joey's apartment, we could find out what Walt was referring to, and maybe it was something innocent. Oh, come on. You are the world's biggest snoop. You've done things like this before, don't tell me you haven't. I'll never forget how you set me up to distract poor unsuspecting Mae Mae and Lucy Lou while you went snooping around Mae Mae's house, stealing the poor woman's diary, for pity sakes!"

Well, she had me there. "Okay," I said. "I'll help you. But what do you care? Joey's gone. What difference does it make."

She replied, "I don't like them sullying his good name."

"If he had a good name," I mumbled under my breath.

The police had sealed Joey's apartment door with crime scene tape. Yellow tape that said "POLICE LINE - DO NOT CROSS." We were standing on the second floor landing outside his apartment wondering what to do next.

"Does your plan include how we are going to get inside?" I asked.

"Hmmm. Well, I thought something would occur to us once we got here. Like, maybe, going to the manager's office and saying we're a housekeeping crew, something like that."

I gave her a head to toe. "Yes, we do look like Merry Maids, don't we? You in that outfit and me in construction boots. Let's switch to plan B. Which is . . . ?"

"See if those bimbos next door have a key?" Melanie tapped on the door across the landing.

We waited. No one came to the door. "Probably gone home for winter break," I said. "They looked like freshmen to me."

I walked back to Joey's door and stared at it. "Okay, let's try the obvious." I reached in through the yellow tape X and gave the door knob a turn. We both gasped when it turned all the way and the door opened.

"Yikes! Now what?" I had not expected to succeed.

Quickly Melanie loosened the tape at the bottom of the door, lifted it, and pushed me inside. "Sometimes you think too much."

We stood inside a tiny foyer. The light was very dim. She closed the door behind us and pressed the thumb latch. "We don't want to be interrupted," she said. "Go on."

I took a step further into the apartment. A galley kitchen opened into the foyer. Beyond that was the living room and we entered it next. The lights were out and even though it was still daylight outside, the interior of the apartment was dim. The only light came from a gurgling fish tank with fish floating on top of the water, belly up. "Oh, poor babies," I said. "No one fed them. Well, that explains the funny smell. Did you know he had fish? Were you ever here before, Melanie?"

"Never," she said.

"Well, where did you . . . ? You know. Last summer?"

"My house on Sandpiper Cove. While the rest of you were at the beach house." She didn't sound proud, I will give her that.

"I don't want to talk about that. I'm ashamed of the things I've done in the past. I'm a new person. From now on, I am behaving differently where men are concerned," she assured me.

I gave her a little hug. "I'm proud of you. And you've always been so ethical in business. It was only with men that

199

you lost your head."

"I know. I confess. But they're all so cute, Ashley. I love'em all."

"Okay, Mel. So what are we looking for?"

"I don't know. Something to confirm my faith in Joey. That he wasn't involved in anything underhanded. Something to reassure me that my judgement was not all bad. I know — oh, I know — if we had looked closely at Mickey, we'd have found worms in the larder — that's why I broke it off with him. But not Joey."

"Look, Mel, Mickey had something going when he was killed. He told me someone owed him a lot of money and he was not leaving town until he collected. And you can be sure the money was not legitimately earned."

"Okay, well, here's Joey's desk. Let's go through the drawers. See what's there." She pulled out the middle drawer.

Seeing detached cables under the desk, I said, "Oh, look, the cops must have taken his computer. See, its gone."

"And there's not much of anything in these desk drawers. The police must have acted on Walt's suggestion that Joey was involved in something illegal and seized his papers. Wonder what they took."

I moved back into the foyer. "I'm ready to get out of here. The cops might come back. I don't want to get caught here."

"I don't think they'll be back soon. They affixed that yellow tape," Melanie suggested.

"Well, why didn't they lock the door?" I asked.

She shrugged. "Maybe they thought they did. Come on, we'll just take a quick peek in the bedroom since we're already here. Then we'll leave." She sighed heavily. "Maybe this wasn't such a good idea after all. I don't know what I expected to find here."

She walked down a hallway that led to an open doorway. It had to be the bedroom, it was the only room left.

When she reached the doorway she froze and breathed out a sharp, "No!"

"What?" I squealed and hurried to catch up.

She turned quickly and seized me by the shoulders, propelling me backward down the hall. "Don't look. Don't look."

"What is it? What, Mel?"

Her wide eyes met mine. "It's Ali Shariff. He's been shot in the head, just like Joey! Come on we're getting out of here. I'm already in enough trouble. I'm not going to be blamed for this." She was yanking tissues out of her purse, using them to seize the door knob. She pushed me out the door and onto the landing before I could utter a single protest. Then used the tissues to wipe the door knob and the outside of the door.

"But he could be alive," I argued.

"No. He definitely could not!"

30

"I can't believe we left Ali that way," I told Melanie.

It was the Saturday afternoon after Thanksgiving, and we were strolling around Festival in the Park at the Wrightsville Beach Municipal Park. There were booths, live music, rides for kids, an art show. The booths featured hand-made crafts and works of art by local artisans. Melanie had already filled two shopping bags with Christmas presents and I was catching up fast.

"That was the nicest Thanksgiving we've had since Daddy died. With Aunt Ruby and Binkie, Cam and Jon, it's like we have a family again. But, oh! I miss Mama and Daddy so much."

"So do I, shug, but they'd want us to be happy, and to love the folks that have been sent into our lives."

I gave her a startled look. "God, Melanie, you have changed."

"Well, I could have died. That was a wake up call. Was I really that bad?"

"No. Never. Not when the chips were down. But other times, you did have an attitude," I confessed. "This new you is going to take some getting used to."

"Oh, look!" she cried, stopping at a leather works craft booth. "A tool belt. I have to confess, Ashley, I've always envied you wearing that macho tool belt of yours, but look at this one. It's girly!"

"I painted those flowers myself," the lady inside the booth said proudly, and lifted the leather belt to show off her handiwork. The pale leather of the tool belt was decorated with colorful flowers, and the handles of the hammer and other tools were painted with similar flowers.

Melanie lifted it and held it around her waist. "What do you think?" she asked me. "My new look."

"You know I approve. Every woman needs to learn how to handle a tool," I replied.

She wagged her eyebrows at me.

"Don't even think of saying it," I said but grinned.

Melanie said to the painter, "I'll take it, but do you have a sturdy shopping bag to hold it?"

The woman rolled the tool belt into a tight bundle. "This heavy plastic bag will carry it just fine."

Melanie took the bag but looked weighed down. "Here," I said, taking one of the other shopping bags from her, "I'll carry this in my good arm. I'm lucky my right arm was not injured when I fell."

We passed by food booths with their savory smells. I said, "I'm still full from Thanksgiving dinner. I couldn't do justice to that spread we were served last night at the kick-off party at the Blockade Runner."

"You're losing weight, baby sis, and you look better than I've ever seen you look. The right man is good for a woman's appearance. And good sex will make your skin glow like no expensive beauty product." She gave me a wry smile. "I like the way you're wearing your hair a little longer. See, I told you that letting it grow would draw out some of that curl. Now you've got soft waves. Very pretty."

"Good sex, huh? And is that why your skin looks so smooth and clear? You know everything, don't you, big sis?" But I laughed.

The temperatures had dropped from near summer-like record highs and we both had on jeans and suede jackets. But the air was dry and the sun was warm.

"Well, I do know a lot when it comes to fashion and hair styles. Comes from my beauty pageant days. And I knew the police would find Ali without our involving ourselves and me getting accused of murder again. Gosh, I wish they'd catch this killer and let me off the hook. Sometimes I swear they're following me. Like now."

We both turned around but didn't see a person we recognized or anyone who was acting suspiciously. A lot of moms and dads and little tykes, seniors with stuffed shopping bags like ours.

"I don't see anyone," I said.

"I know. I never see anyone either, but I could swear someone is there. The hair on the back of my neck gets all prickly and I get goosely bumps. It's an instinctive reaction we humans have left over from our cave man days when we were stalked by predators."

"That's exactly how I felt right before that guy attacked me in the park. There is a predator out on the loose, that's for sure," I said. "I have to tell you, I know who had a strong motive for killing Ali. David Boleyn!"

I told Melanie all about seeing Crystal and Ali together at Prima's restaurant. "And the way they were glued at the hips on the cruise! They were almost daring him to react."

"Well, why wouldn't he just divorce Crystal? Wouldn't that be simpler? And maybe that's why she's been flaunting Ali in front of him. To get him to let her go. He's mighty possessive. After all, she told us she had a pre-nup. He doesn't have a thing to loose," Melanie argued.

"Only his pride," I said, "and the man's an egomaniac."

"What about Clay Bitterman? Ali was giving Brie a hard time about something. Maybe it was him. Protecting his little girl. Or just a quarrel that got out of control."

"I can't see Clay Bitterman pulling the trigger, can you?" I asked. "He just doesn't have it in him."

"We all have it in us. But why were they in Joey's apartment if it was Clay? Why meet there?"

"I don't know. The police told me Ali lived in the same complex. Did he and Joey know each other? Maybe he had a key to Joey's apartment."

"Not that I know of. And Ali was on tour with Brie during the summer when I was . . . uh . . . seeing Joey. What were Brie and Ali fighting about anyway? Do you know? He's been with her from day one," Melanie said.

"And that's what it's about," I replied. "I think she's dropping him and changing managers. He was pretty upset about it."

"And what about that so-called ATF agent who's been prowling around in the background and who followed you into the park? There's something fishy about that guy. Walt was never able to confirm that he was legit and that there was an ATF agent here on special assignment. So maybe he's not who he says he is," Melanie speculated.

"And maybe some one flashed a phony badge and lied to the gardeners to get inside the park," I reasoned. "They're gardeners, what would they know about whether a badge is authentic or not. I didn't."

"But why attack you? What could you possibly know?" she asked. "Listen, it's time for us to leave. We've got to meet Cam and Jon at the boat so we can get in the parade. Those sweet guys have spent the whole day decorating the boat and I can't . . . What? What's wrong? Do you see someone?"

I had come to an abrupt halt. One of the vendors was flattening boxes and I flashed back to dreams I'd been having. Dreams about boxes. On the sides of the boxes words had been stamped but when I focussed on them to read them, the letters got all blurry and I couldn't see what they said.

I turned to give her a puzzled look. "Melanie, David says Crystal is redecorating the lower deck of the yacht and that's why the staterooms were filled with boxes and why he didn't want us going down there."

"Yes," Melanie said pensively, picking up on my strange vibes. "And . . . ?"

"Well, it just doesn't make sense."

"Tell me what you're thinking," she said. We had stopped walking and were face to face, her eyes looking questioningly into mine. Crowds milled around us.

"It's just that the staterooms are furnished with built-in's. You can't just rip them out on your own and replace them with loose furniture. You're going to have to take the ship back to the manufacturer or to a yacht servicing company. It's not like replacing the furniture in your home. And the shades and headliners are all custom made articles. Crystal just can't set up a sewing machine and run up a pair of draperies for the guest stateroom."

"You're right about that, little girl," David Boleyn said with a sneer from behind Melanie. "I've got a gun in her back. So turn around and start walking. My car's right over there."

31

"Oh, my God, what have you done to Crystal Lynne!" Melanie screamed, dropping her shopping bags and racing to the king-sized berth where Crystal lay sprawled.

"Gave her what she deserved. Little tramp," David sneered. "You two are next, soon's this stupid parade is over and we can break out of this carnival."

"What are you going to do to us?" I asked.

David detected the fear in my voice because he said, "I knew this experience would take you down a peg or two, little girl."

I never realized before just how ugly David Boleyn really was. Mean, with cold beady eyes, and that constant sneer.

"This boat is sea worthy and we're going out to sea soon's I can pilot her out of this damn line-up. Once we're out at sea, well, accidents do happen at sea. You three little girls are going to end up as fish food." He threw back his head and snorted.

"There's two of us, Ashley!" Melanie screamed. "Let's rush him."

She started for him across the stateroom. I ran at him

from the other direction. He just grinned and fired a warning shot into the padded headliner. That stopped us. "Not a good idea," he said flatly.

We could only look helplessly at each other.

David marched across the stateroom and yanked the telephone out of the wall. "Okay, now hand over your cell phones. I've already got Crystal's."

He held out his free hand and took the cell phones Melanie and I dragged out of our purses, then stuffed them in the pockets of his baggy pants.

"What's in those bags?" he asked suspiciously.

"Christmas presents," I said in a whisper.

He turned to leave. "You girls have fun in here," he laughed as he stepped into the companionway. He closed the bi-fold doors behind him and locked them shut from the outside. I heard the distinct sound of a key turning in the lock.

Melanie was staring down at Crystal. "Look at her. He really beat her up bad. I think she's got a broken jaw."

Melanie sat down on the bed and felt Crystal's neck for a pulse. Then she began to pat Crystal's wrist. "Crystal Lynne, wake up, honey." To me she said, "She's alive but she's out cold. Ashley, go into the bathroom and run cold water on some hand towels and bring them to me."

Melanie used a wet towel to gently wipe the dried blood from Crystal's nose and lips. She draped the other wet towel on Crystal's forehead. "I think he broke her jaw. That's what knocked her out. She needs medical help."

"*We* need help, Melanie. We've got to get out of here!" I said.

Melanie turned to look at the portlights. "Well, those portholes are too small for us to crawl through."

I stared at the bi-fold door that led to the companionway. "I'm getting us out of here. But we've got to wait until the fireworks start. I need the noise as cover."

"What are you going to do?" Melanie asked.

"I'm going to dismantle that door!"

"But, how . . . oh, you are a genius."

The yacht was floating now, underway. The Holiday Flotilla had begun, one hundred plus boats parading from the starting point at the Wrightsville Drawbridge, slowly sailing along Motts Channel to Banks Channel and south. Melanie and I raced to the portholes to look out. There was a nautical light show on the water, and holiday music that could be heard even here inside.

The boats were decorated with thousands of lights, many had themes, like the Cat in the Hat sail boat. Smaller, spectator vessels hugged the shores, and fifty thousand people lined the banks, watching, cheering. We should have been on Cam's boat, enjoying all of this too. Instead we were trapped with a psychopathic killer and wife beater.

"I think we're safe for now," I said. "He's kind of trapped in the parade. He won't be able to sail out until the parade is over and the boats anchor to watch the fireworks. Even then, he may be hemmed in, this yacht is so big."

As we stared out the portholes at flashing lights reflecting on the black water, Crystal moaned from the bed.

"She's coming to," Melanie said.

We both ran to the berth. "Crystal Lynne, honey, wake up," Melanie said, sitting down beside her and lifting her hand.

"Ummmm," she murmured and fluttered her eyelids.

"It's Melanie, sugar. Ashley's here too. We're going to get you out of here. Away from that monster."

Crystal's eyes flew open in terror. "David," she mumbled. "Ouch." Tears flooded her eyes.

Melanie turned to me. "She can't talk with that broken jaw." To Crystal she said, "I know it's hard for you to talk but we have to know. Did David kill all those people? Joey? Mickey? Ali? Just squeeze my hand if the answer is yes."

Crystal squeezed Melanie's hand. "Just as I thought,"

Melanie said, looking up at me from the bed.

"But why, Crystal Lynne? What's going on here? He wants to kill us too, you know." She flashed me a look of admiration. "But Ashley won't let him. Ashley's going to get us out of here. My little sister has more guts and brains than the two of us put together."

"Smuggling," Crystal mumbled, but it came out sounding like "schmuglin." "Cigarettes," she whispered harshly. "Joey. Mickey."

"Oh my gosh!" I cried. "The boxes! That explains it. My dream. I saw the boxes, then dreamt about seeing words stamped on the boxes. That day I was seasick, I got only a glimpse of them. And there were words stamped on the boxes. The brand names of cigarettes."

"Ashley, I think you should get started on those doors. I don't think he'll be able to hear all the way up on the fly-bridge with the music and the noise of the crowd."

"I think you're right," I said and lifted the heavy plastic bag to the bed. Melanie was trying to get Crystal to sip some water but most of the water just ran down her chin.

I removed a hammer and a collection of screwdrivers from Melanie's cutesy tool belt. The belt might look feminine with all the cute flowers painted on it but it held the usual variety of tools.

The bi-fold doors were held together with polished nickel hinges set on the inside. Lucky for us. Removing hinges from a door, especially new doors like these where there was no build up of dirt or paint, was a piece of cake. I inserted the tip of the screwdriver's blade at the base of the hinge pin and tapped it with the hammer.

The pin moved up slowly. When about an inch of it protruded from the hinge, I grasped it with pliers and pulled it out.

"How's it going?" Melanie asked.

"A breeze," I replied. "How is she?"

"She's more alert." To Crystal, she said, "Here, sweetie, let me slip another pillow under your head and sit you up."

The hinge at the bottom is always the hardest because it is near the floor and there is a small amount of space between it and the floor. I had to use the tiniest screwdriver with the shortest handle, and even then it was difficult to fit the hammer under it. But desperation is the ultimate motivator, and within minutes I had the lower pin out.

I moved upward to the top hinge. I am five-five and was able to reach and remove the top hinge easily. Then, using the screwdriver with the longest, thinnest blade, I inserted the blade between the door panels and prized the outer panel open. Plenty of space for we three slim women to squeeze through and out into the empty companionway.

Melanie was helping Crystal off the bed. Crystal was gesturing frantically, trying to communicate something to Melanie. Staggering to her feet, she lumbered into the bathroom.

"What a time to have to go," Melanie complained bitterly.

But Crystal had something else in mind. Through the open door we watched as she picked up a large size vinyl make-up bag and dumped the contents into the sink bowl. On unsteady legs, she wobbled back into the stateroom and knelt in front of one of the lower built-in cabinets. She opened the door, and inside there was the door to a safe.

Crystal knew the combination. She spun the dial — left, then right, then left again — grasped the handle and pulled the thick door open. Money, stacks of money filled the safe. She stuffed bundles of bills into her make-up bag until it could hold no more.

Then she gave us a look. She was ready.

About the same time, the boat stopped moving. The parade part of the festival was over. Now the fireworks would start. And they began immediately with a pop, pop, pop.

"Come on," I called. "With the boat at anchor, he doesn't need to stay on the flybridge. He'll be back down here and who knows what he'll do to us. I just hope the boat is hemmed in so he can't set sail into open waters where he'll have us alone."

One by one we passed through the opening in the door into the companionway.

"The sport deck," Crystal said. Only it came out of her mouth sounding like, "Ta spor da." She winced when she spoke. She had more courage than I had given her credit for.

The sport deck was located aft on this level but access to it was blocked by the engine room.

We ran single-file through the companionway, up the stairway, and into the salon. We fled through it to the sliding glass doors. Pulling them open, we stepped onto the aft deck. Melanie had the good sense to slide the door shut after us.

Out here the lights from the boats and the fireworks were bright, and reflecting off the water as they did, there was plenty of light to see around us. We were surrounded by boats with large parties of revelers on the open decks.

I nudged Melanie. "Look!" I cried. The nearest boat was the *Hot Momma*. Jon! And Cam. I waved to them but they were staring up into the sky at the exploding fireworks as was everyone else.

We raced down the outside stairway to the sport deck. This was the deck used for fishing and water skiing.

"We're going to swim to that boat," I yelled to Crystal and pointed to the *Hot Momma*.

The water would be cold but the distance was short. We'd be sure to attract attention and get the help we needed.

Melanie counted to three and dived off the sport deck into the water. I followed and hoped Crystal would jump too. If she did not, there wasn't much we could do about it.

The water around us began to roil. What? It took a second for me to realize that bullets were striking the water around us. And then Melanie was screaming and grabbing her arm.

I swam alongside her. "I'm hit," she cried. "My arm."

"Roll onto your back," I said. "Float, and I'll tow you."

I wrapped an arm under her chin and towed her along my right side as I stroked the water with my free arm and kicked with both feet. We were closing the distance between the *Crystal Lynne* and the *Hot Momma*.

As with a soldier in heated battle, for me everything seemed to be happening in slow motion and all my senses were heightened. I was aware of the chill of the water, of its brackish smell, the fireworks popping above us in the sky, the lights from the boats shimmering on the inky water.

I heard Jon's cry. I looked up and saw him pointing to the *Crystal Lynne*. I looked too. Crystal had not jumped into the water. She and David were struggling over something. At first I thought it was the vinyl bag with the money but I had seen Crystal tuck that into her waist band. No, they were struggling over the gun.

There were more popping noises that seemed to be distinct from the fireworks. After that, both Crystal and David fell to the floor of the sport deck and disappeared from view.

By then Jon and Cam had spotted us and were in the water swimming toward us. And off to the Wilmington shore, a man dove off a Coast Guard vessel and began paddling toward us too. Agent Scott Randolph.

Jon, Cam and Agent Randolph got Melanie and me safely aboard the *Hot Momma*. Blankets were wrapped around us and hot coffee from a thermos poured into us.

We all stared at the sport deck of the *Crystal Lynne* where no one remained standing. A shrill toot and boats parted, allowing the Coast Guard vessel to bear down on the *Crystal Lynne*.

32

Christmas Eve

"Your tree is beautiful," Crystal said.

"It's nice to have only one tree to decorate and water," I said. "Two years ago when this house was on the Candlelight Tour, I had five of them. Five! How are you feeling, Crystal? I notice you're speaking almost normally."

"They took the wires out of my jaw last week. What a relief. It's nice to be able to talk again," she replied.

"I'd never be able to keep my mouth shut for almost a month," Melanie said with a grin.

"You are so good to let me live with you in your beautifully redecorated house while I'm sorting things out, Melanie," Crystal said.

We were gathered in my red library. Jon was mixing and serving Cosmopolitan Martinis blended with vodka, Cointreau, lime juice, and cranberry juice.

Binkie took a sip and laughed, "This is a potent drink, Jon. I just might be seeing two Santas tonight."

"Well, we're not driving," Aunt Ruby said.

She and Binkie were spending Christmas with me, and then Melanie and I with Jon and Cam were going with them to Savannah for New Years. One evening when I got home from work there had been a message on my answering machine from Nick saying he hoped I was well and that he wished me a merry Christmas. Nick has my cell phone number so apparently he really didn't want to speak directly to me but merely wanted to wish me well. At least, that was how I was taking it and I was happy to realize that hearing his voice did not cause me to feel any pangs of unrequited love.

Binkie said, "We are so grateful you and Melanie escaped unharmed from David Boleyn. The man was a psychopath. When I think of what might have happened if you hadn't kept your head, Ashley, well . . . thank God you are all right. I'd like to hear the details of his crimes."

"I think I'll let Scott tell you just what David Boleyn was up to," I replied.

Agent Scott Randolph was in Wilmington visiting a friend and had called. When I invited him to our little Christmas Eve party he seemed happy to accept. The last time I had seen him had been Thanksgiving weekend. He had been quick to assure me that it was not he who had followed me into Airlie Gardens and attacked me. "That was Boleyn with a phony badge, hoping to silence you because you had seen the boxes."

Now he explained, "David Boleyn was using his yacht and his contacts and knowledge of how the tobacco industry worked to receive cigarettes stolen from warehouses in southern states and smuggle them to northern and western states where the taxes were highest. The crime is called buttlegging. Once there, the cigarettes were sold through illegal channels for less than the market rate but still high enough to yield a large profit for the smugglers and the middlemen."

"But David wasn't in it for the money," Crystal said. "David had made millions on his own. He didn't need money from smuggling cigarettes. He was doing it because he detested the federal government and the way they taxed cigarettes and how hard they were trying to put the tobacco companies out of business."

Aunt Ruby said to Crystal sympathetically, "But your husband did kill Joey Fielding and Mickey Ballantine. And Ali Shariff. Isn't that so?"

Crystal nodded and seemed to be ashamed that she had been married to such a man.

"We can only guess at his motives," Scott said, "even though there has been a full investigation. Joey Fielding had been working with David Boleyn, providing his restaurant as a place for the trucks to deliver cartons of contraband cigarettes during the dead of night. The cartons were then loaded onto Boleyn's yacht which was tied up at the restaurant's boat dock."

Melanie gasped. "I saw one of those trucks. I thought it was a food delivery truck."

Scott continued, "That's what Fielding wanted everyone to think and they did and that's why the plan worked."

"How was Mickey Ballantine involved?" Cam asked.

"Again we can't be certain, but we think that Ballantine was helping in some way and that he wanted more money — or maybe he threatened to go to the authorities if he didn't get more money — so Boleyn silenced him. Ballantine may have even thought he could cut a deal and have his charges reduced in exchange for information about the smuggling ring."

"But I remember Boleyn saying he was out at sea during the day of the murder," Jon said.

"He wasn't," Crystal said. "He made me lie for him. We were in port. I was with Ali and David used that against me to make me lie for him. I swear, you've got to believe me, I didn't know until the very end that David had killed anybody.

I knew he was bribing elected officials, but he told me the cartons of cigarettes were gifts for political friends."

Melanie patted her shoulder. "We believe you, honey bunch. Just look at what that dreadful man did to your pretty face, but you're all healed now, and he's dead and not going to hurt you ever again."

Crystal cried, "I never believed that he'd really try to kill me. I always felt that deep down he really loved me, in his own possessive way. But out on that sport deck, he aimed the gun at me and was actually going to kill me. I struggled with him and it's amazing how strong you can be when you are fighting for your life. The gun seemed to go off by itself."

She sobbed. "I didn't mean to shoot him. I'd never kill anyone. I didn't even know the bullet had struck him. But then we were both down on the decking and he was on top of me with his full body weight. He didn't move. It took one of the coasties to pull him off me."

"Crystal turned over Boleyn's money to the authorities," Scott said. "And she's cooperating with the Justice Department on the bribery scandal."

"She's been completely exonerated," Melanie said. "The police investigated and decided it was self-defense. You had only to look at her to know she was up against a mad man. Why he even shot me!"

"Thank goodness, that was just a superficial wound," Cam said. "And you've had the best plastic surgery, so there might not even be a scar. Not that I'd love her any less if she did have a scar," Cam told us. He was sitting on the arm of Melanie's chair and he leaned in to kiss the top of her head.

Walt Brice had joined our little party as well. "The police are now sharing some information with me about the case," he said. "Joey Fielding had parked his car a few streets over from the Bitterman residence on Point Place. Their guess is that Fielding did not want to drive his new car by the construction that was going on next door, maybe afraid of pick-ing up a roofing nail in his tire. So apparently he arrived at the house on foot, then let Boleyn in. They think Boleyn anchored his yacht in the sound and rode the tender to the Bitterman boat dock. After he killed Fielding, he sailed out into the sound again where he watched for Melanie to arrive. When she did, he called in an anonymous tip to the Wrightsville police, knowing they were only minutes away. By the time they arrived, he was back on the yacht."

Jon said, "He must have used the same M.O. when he met Mickey Ballantine at Melanie's house, both Mickey and Boleyn arriving by small boat."

"Mickey kept the key to Melanie's even when I demand-ed that he give it back to me," I said. "He handed me a bogus key, maybe a key to his old nightclub, who knows?"

Melanie chimed in, "And when David Boleyn heard the garage door open, he knew I had come home. He turned out the lights and waited for me to come in from the garage. Then he knocked me unconscious with my paperweight. Maybe he was trying to kill me, I don't know. But I showed him! I sur-vived! And my hair is growing out nicely. By the time it is long again, David Boleyn will have been forgotten."

Walt said, "The police lab found traces of your hair and blood on the paperweight they took from your house, even though he tried to wipe it clean."

"He killed Ali because of me," Crystal said softly and dropped her chin. "I knew he was jealous but I never dreamt he'd resort to killing. I can't believe Ali is gone, that I'll never see him again." Tears formed in her eyes once more.

"Walt, did you ever find out who Brie Bitterman and her father met with in Charlotte the day Joey was killed?" I asked.

"Our investigator finally pieced that together. Brie is sign-ing up with a major multi-media company. They're working on getting her a TV show and movie contracts. She didn't want Ali to know she was talking to them."

"Does anyone know how David lured Ali to Joey's apartment?" Melanie asked.

Privately, she had confided in me that she didn't know how she had become so besotted with Joey Fielding. She said that now that she was in a real relationship with a man who was her equal, she looked back on that period of her life as an aberration.

"The police don't know how that happened," Walt said. "I'm just glad your name and reputation have been cleared. Your father would have expected no less from me."

"There is one final mystery that I can clear up," Scott Randolph said. "The man you discovered under those antique bottles was my great-grandfather, Silas Randolph, an agent of the Alcohol Tax Unit. A Revenuer, as they were called in those days.

"Dr. McAllister sent our DNA samples to a lab for analysis and the results confirm that we were related. She was also able to determine that he'd been shot in the back. We are assuming by Increase Boleyn or one of his confederates. We'll never know."

"Oh, I'm sorry, Scott," I said. How unsettling it must be to discover that your great-grandfather had been the victim of a murder.

"There will be no justice for my ancestor or for my family," Scott said, "since his murderers are dead now too, but there is a sense of closure. At least now we know how and why he disappeared. Why he never returned home to Georgia."

Melanie clapped her hands. "I think it's time for y'all to hear some good news. Cam and I have an announcement. Crystal Lynne is selling the hunting lodge to us. Ashley and Jon are going to restore it for us. When it's finished, it will be spectacular. They are even going to build a replica of Pembroke Jones's Temple of Love on the estate. And the room with the fireplaces is going to be turned into a fabulous great hall, a perfect place for a wedding next Christmas."

Jon stood up and gave me a questioning look. I nodded my agreement. "A double wedding," he told everyone. He withdrew a small velvet box from his pocket. "Ashley, I was planning to give this to you at midnight. But we're among friends and family. They will all be happy for us."

I stood up next to him and wrapped my arm around his waist. He opened the box, revealing a sparkling diamond engagement ring. I lifted my left hand and he slipped it on my ring finger.

Everyone clapped and cheered. Then he kissed me and I forgot they were there.